COLLECT THE SET!

Boffin Boy and the Invaders from Space
978 184167 613 5

Boffin Boy and the Wizard of Edo
978 184167 614 2

Boffin Boy and the Monsters from the Deep
978 184167 615 9

Boffin Boy and the Red Wolf
978 184167 616 6

Boffin Boy and the Lost City
978 184167 617 3

Boffin Boy and the Time Warriors
978 184167 622 7

Boffin Boy and the Ice Caves of Pluto
978 184167 626 5

Boffin Boy and the Quest for Wisdom
978 184167 628 9

Boffin Boy and the Deadly Swarm
978 184167 625 8

Boffin Boy and the Rock Men
978 184167 624 1

Boffin Boy and the Temples of Mars
978 184167 623 4

Boffin Boy and the Forest of the Ninja
978 184167 627 2

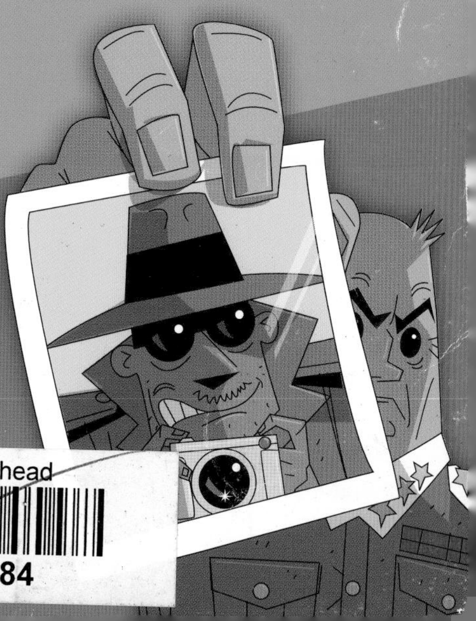

Boffin Boy and the Wizard of Edo
by David Orme

Illustrated by Peter Richardson

Published by Ransom Publishing Ltd.
Radley House, 8 St Cross Road, Winchester, Hants. SO23 9HX
www.ransom.co.uk

ISBN 978 184167 614 2
First published in 2006
Reprinted 2007, 2008, 2011, 2013
Copyright © 2006 Ransom Publishing Ltd.

Illustrations copyright © 2006 Peter Richardson

Design & layout:
www.macwiz.co.uk

Find out more about
Boffin Boy at
www.ransom.co.uk.

Boffin Boy and the Wizard of Edo

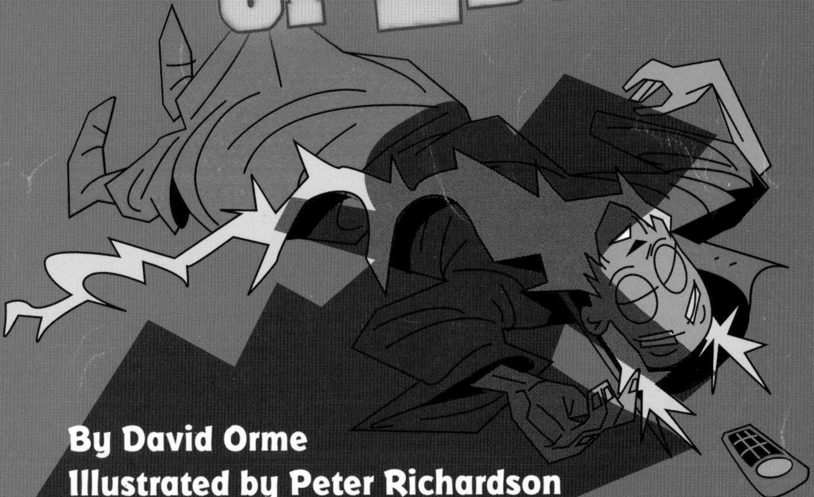

By David Orme
Illustrated by Peter Richardson

Ransom

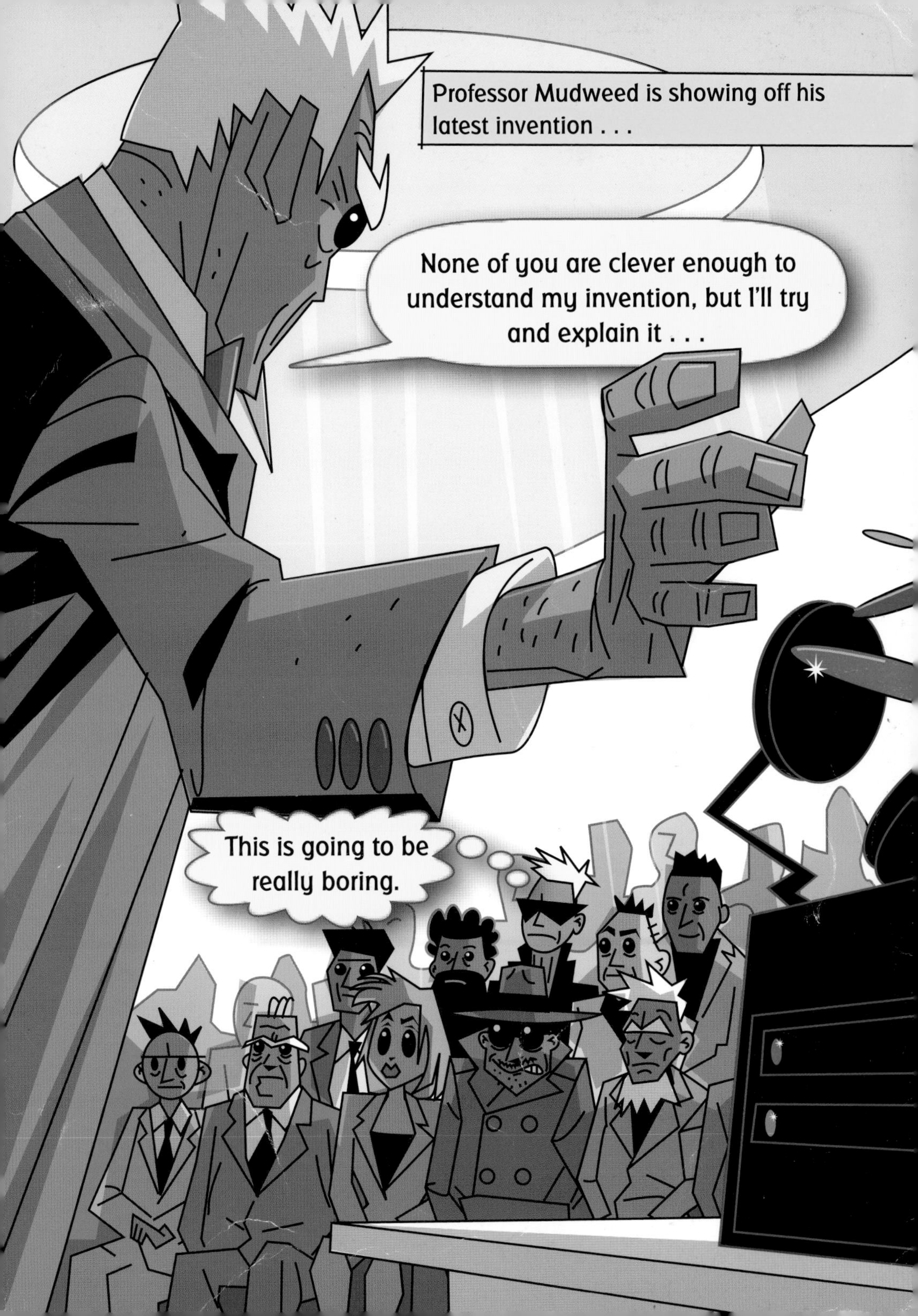
Professor Mudweed is showing off his latest invention . . .
None of you are clever enough to understand my invention, but I'll try and explain it . . .
This is going to be really boring.

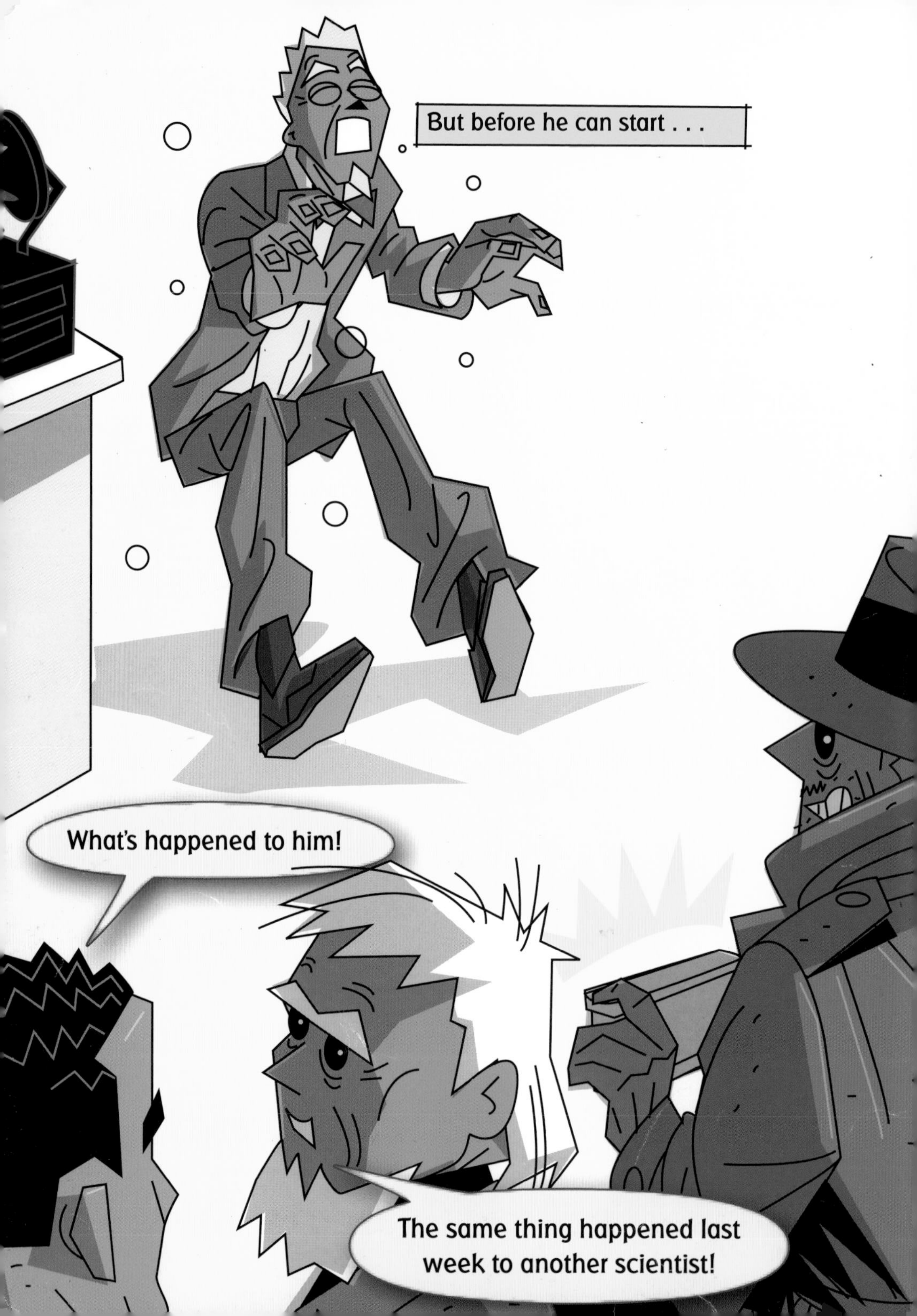
But before he can start . . .
What's happened to him!
The same thing happened last week to another scientist!

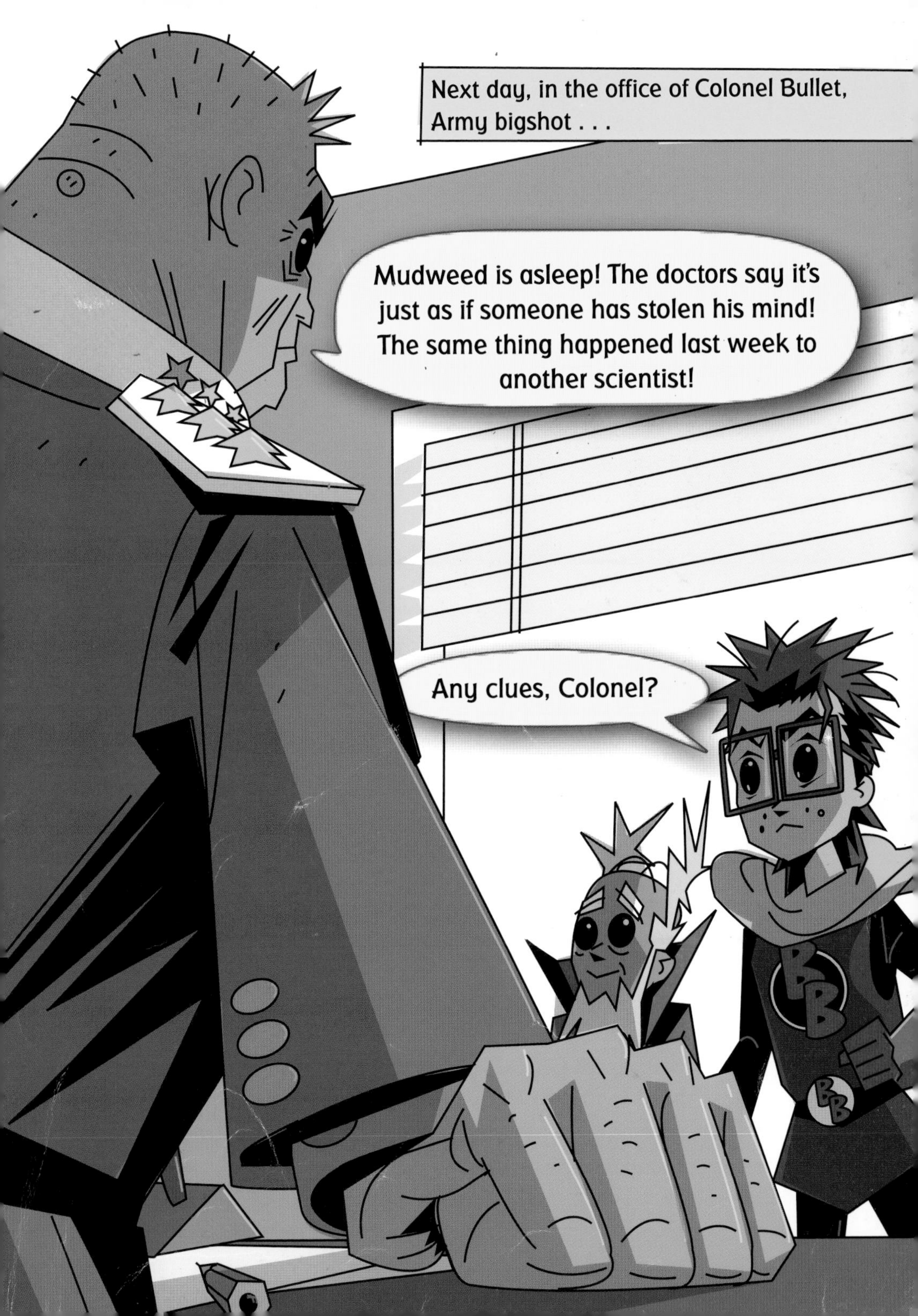
Next day, in the office of Colonel Bullet, Army bigshot . . .
Mudweed is asleep! The doctors say it's just as if someone has stolen his mind! The same thing happened last week to another scientist!
Any clues, Colonel?

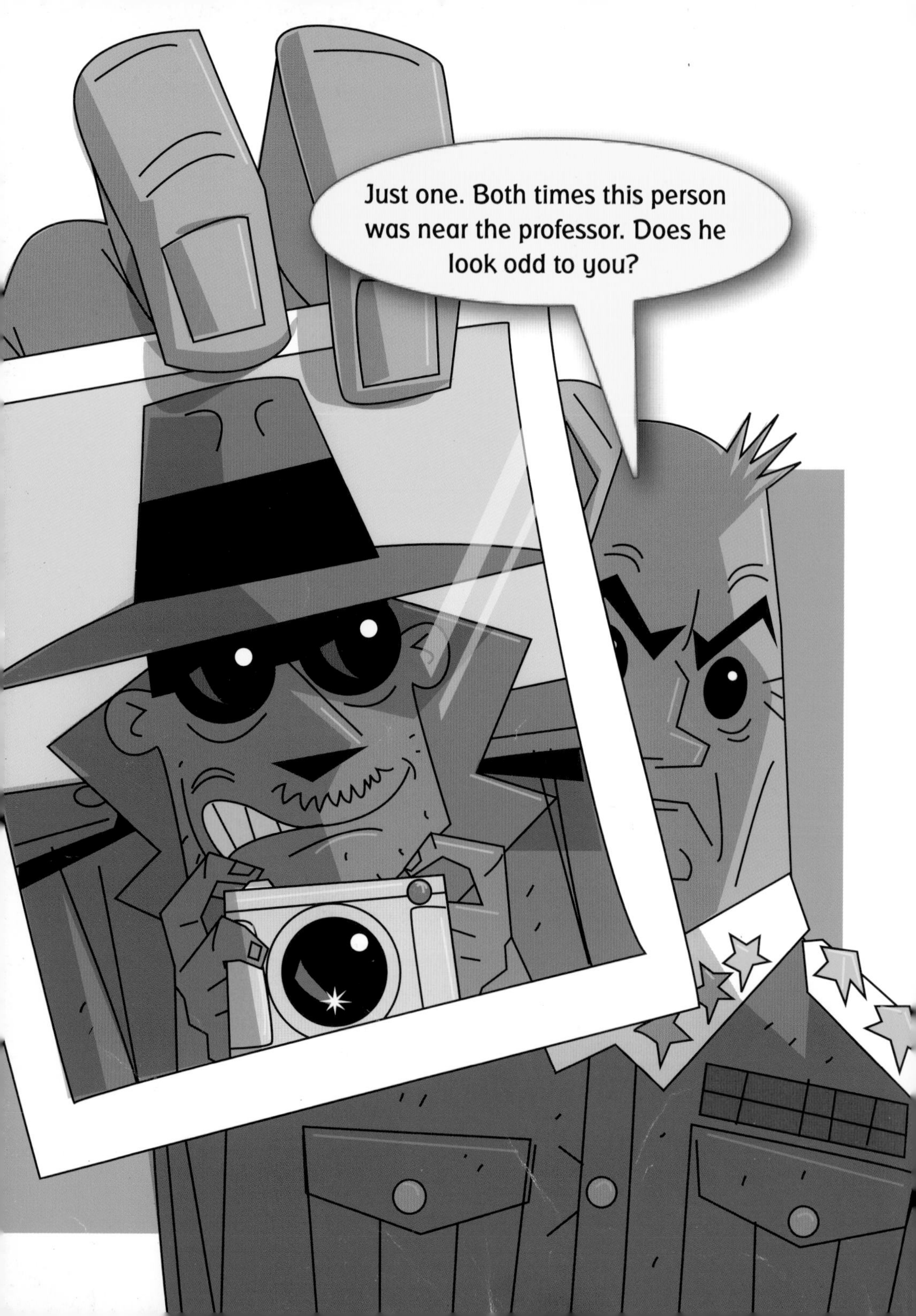
Just one. Both times this person was near the professor. Does he look odd to you?

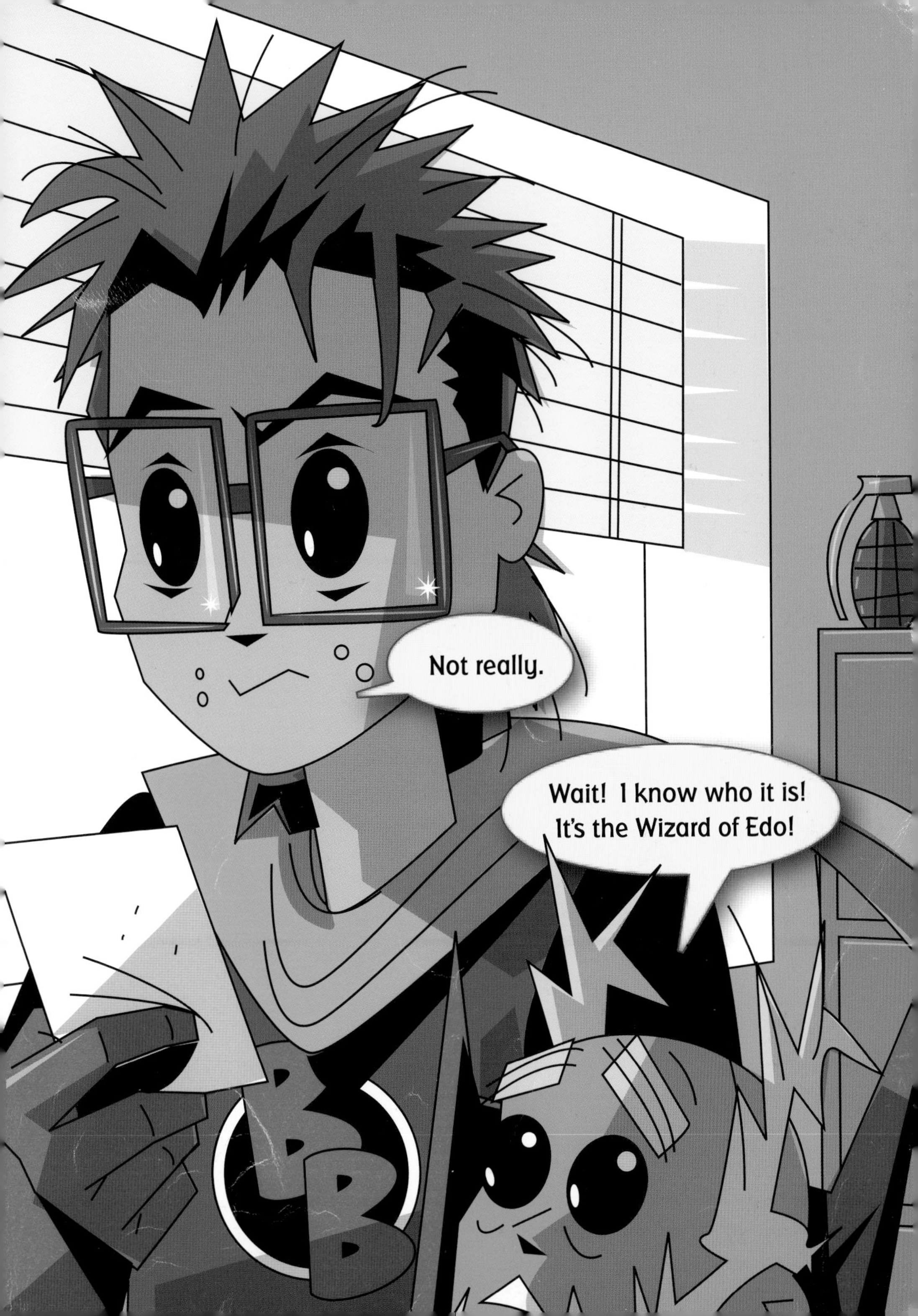
Not really.
Wait! I know who it is! It's the Wizard of Edo!

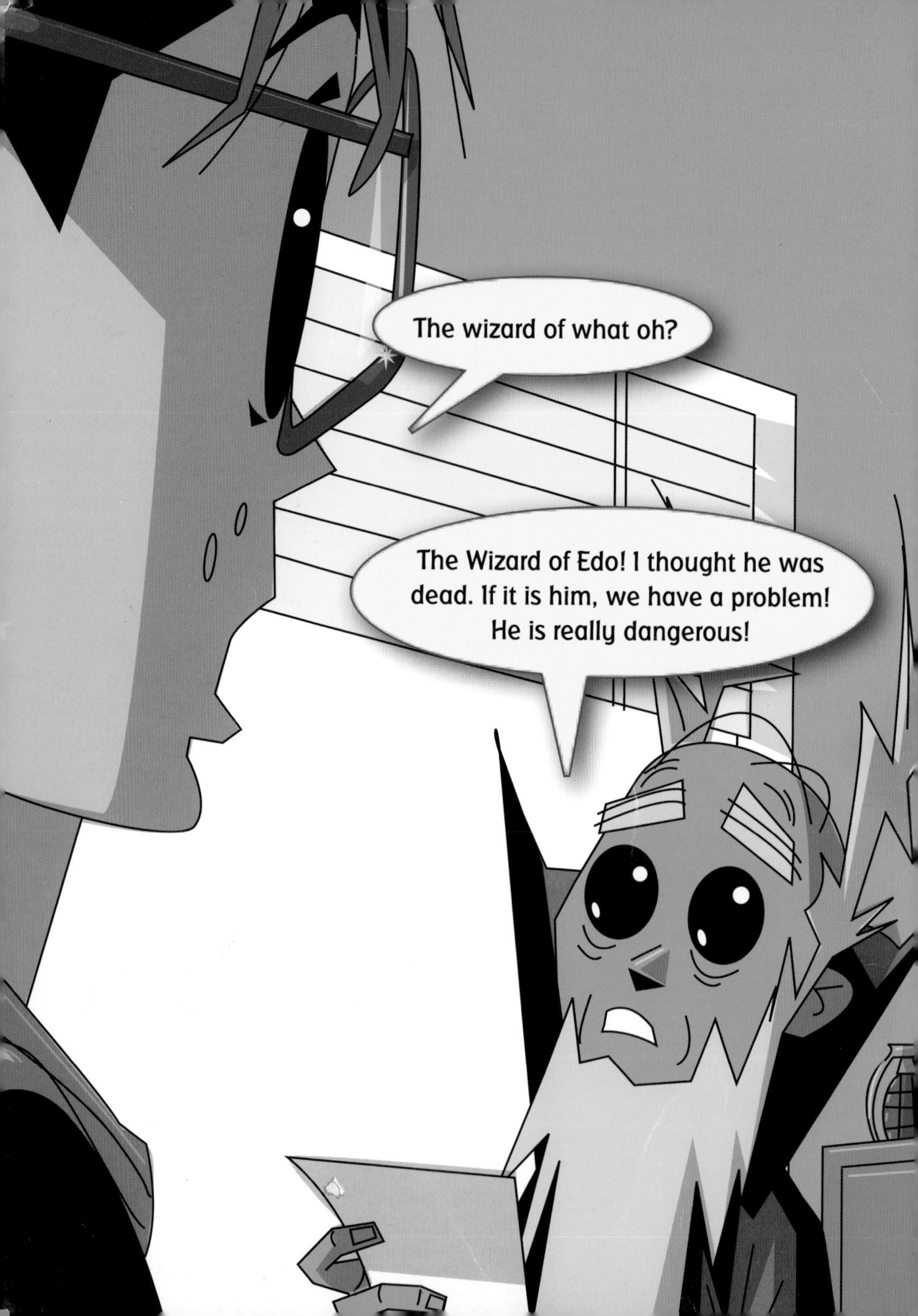
The wizard of what oh?
The Wizard of Edo! I thought he was dead. If it is him, we have a problem! He is really dangerous!

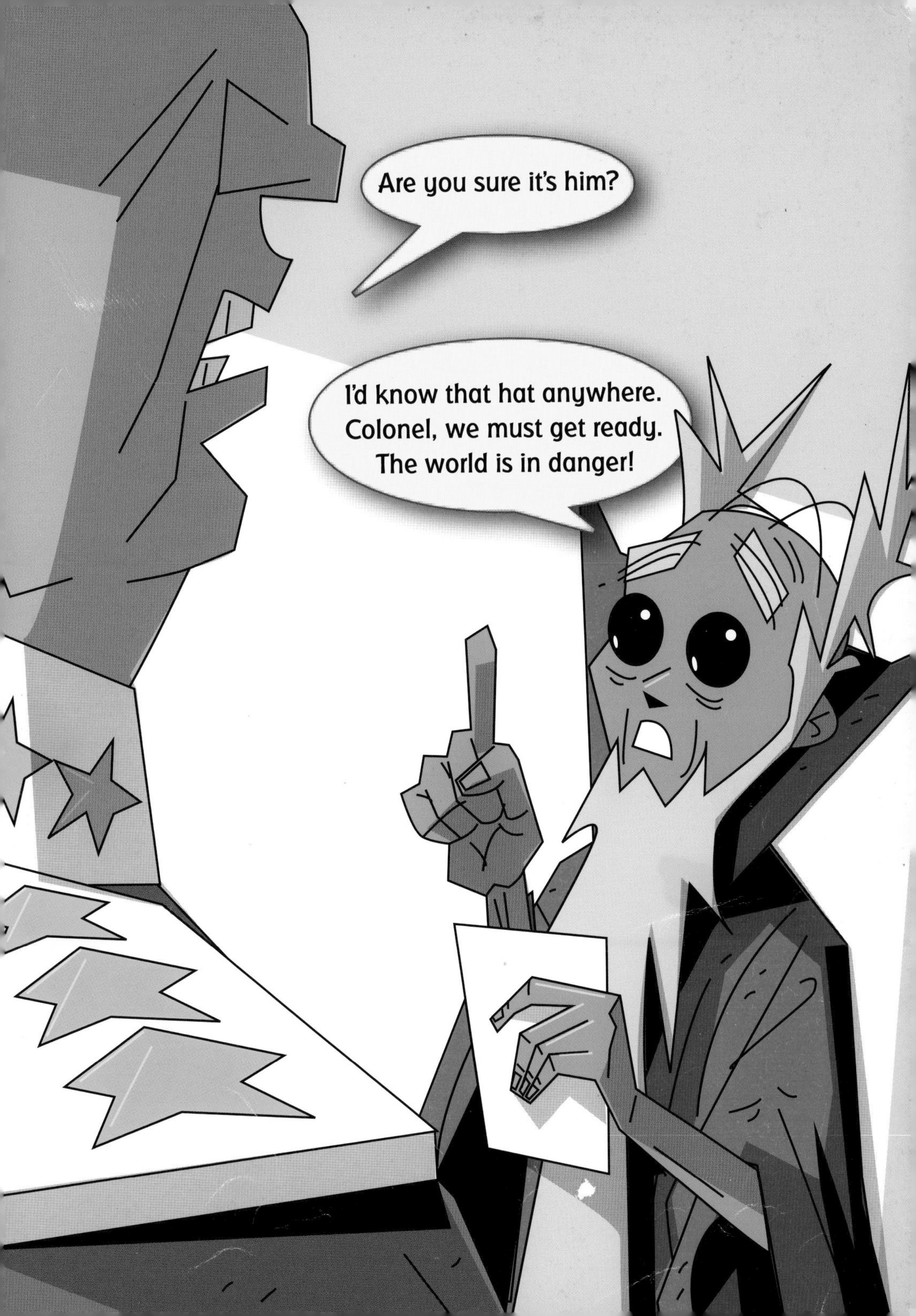
Are you sure it's him?
I'd know that hat anywhere. Colonel, we must get ready. The world is in danger!

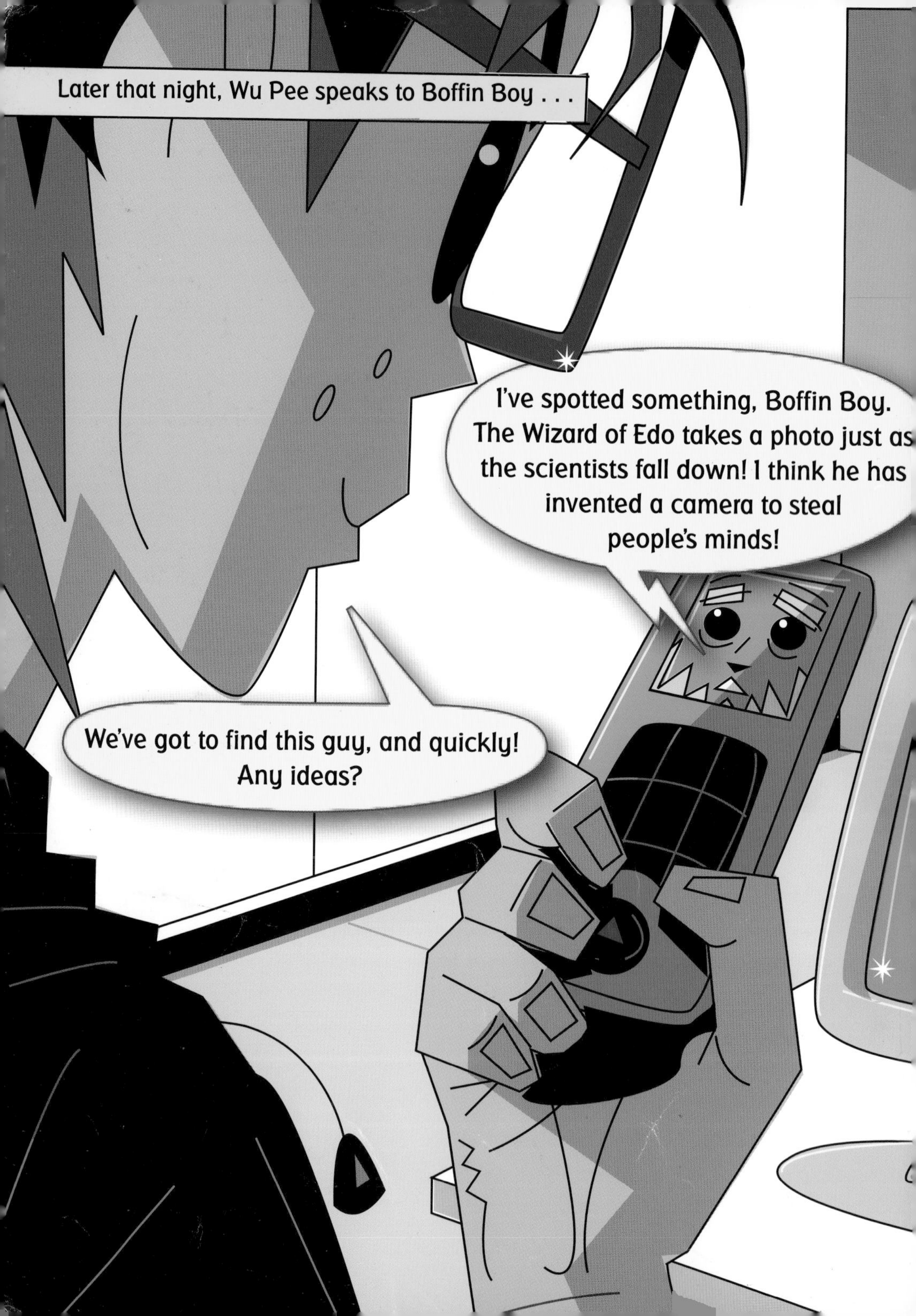
Later that night, Wu Pee speaks to Boffin Boy . . .
I've spotted something, Boffin Boy. The Wizard of Edo takes a photo just as the scientists fall down! I think he has invented a camera to steal people's minds!
We've got to find this guy, and quickly! Any ideas?

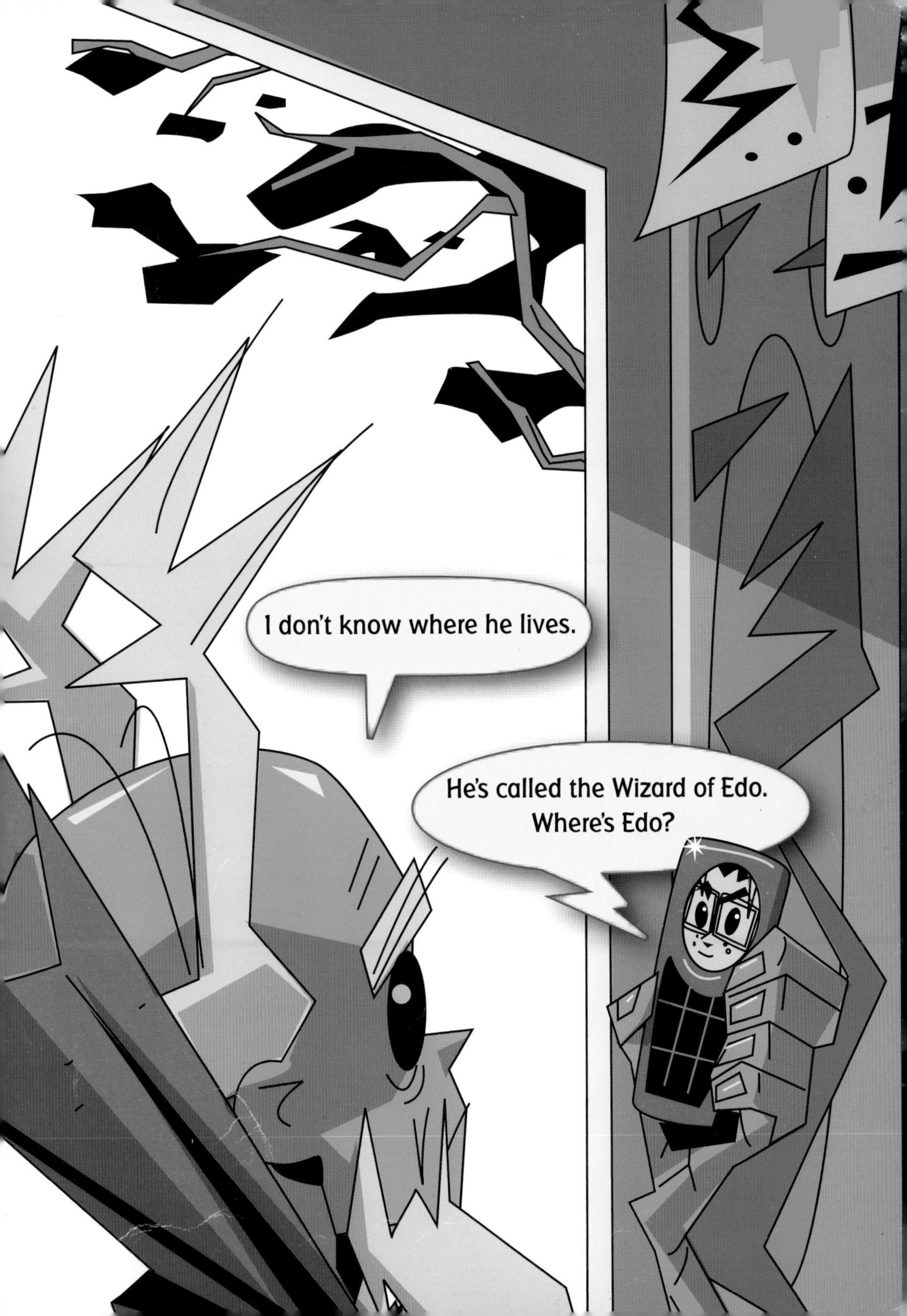
I don't know where he lives.
He's called the Wizard of Edo. Where's Edo?

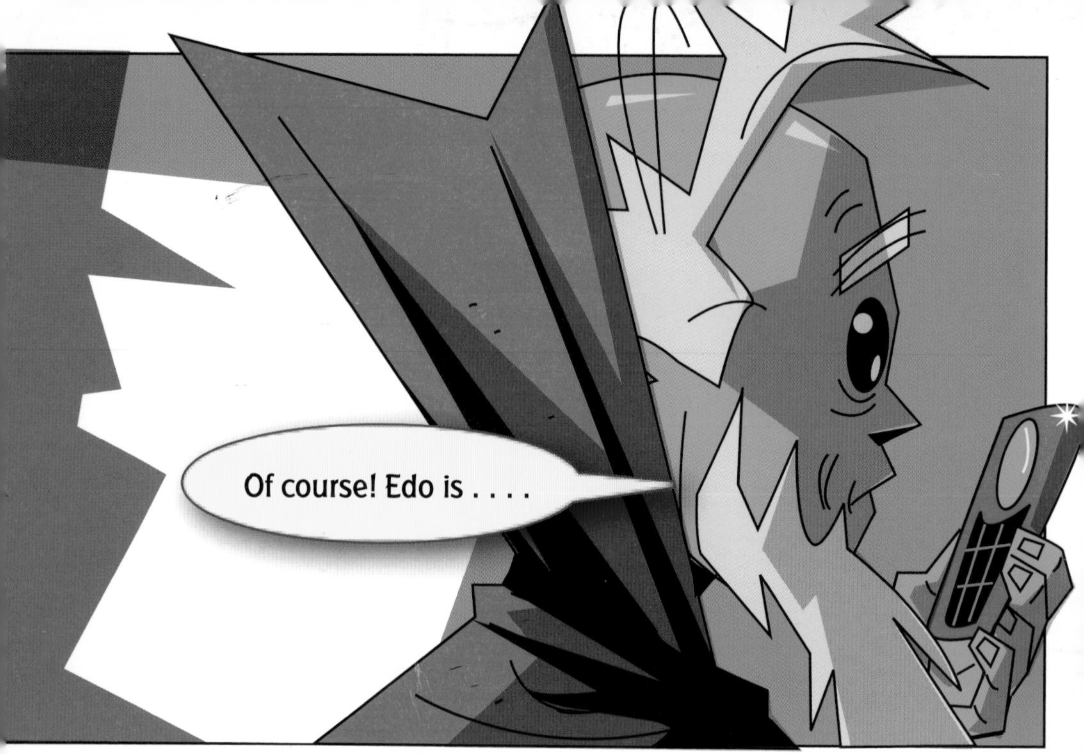
Of course! Edo is . . . .

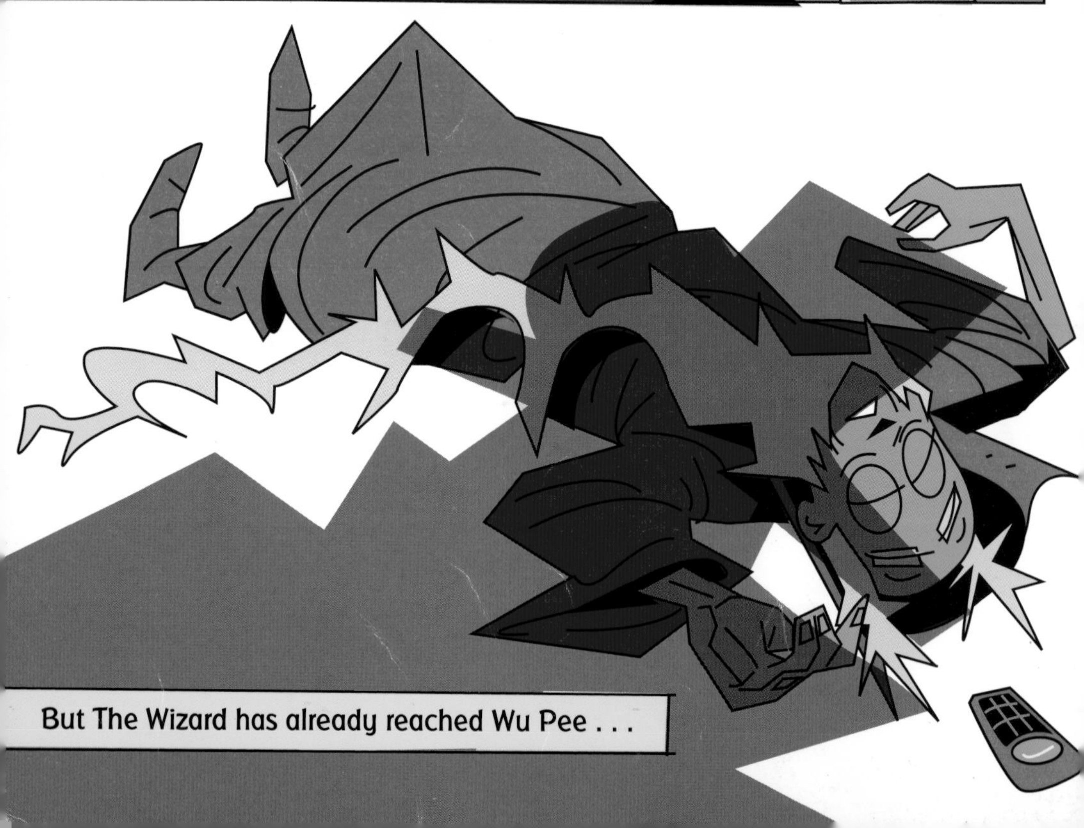
But The Wizard has already reached Wu Pee . . .

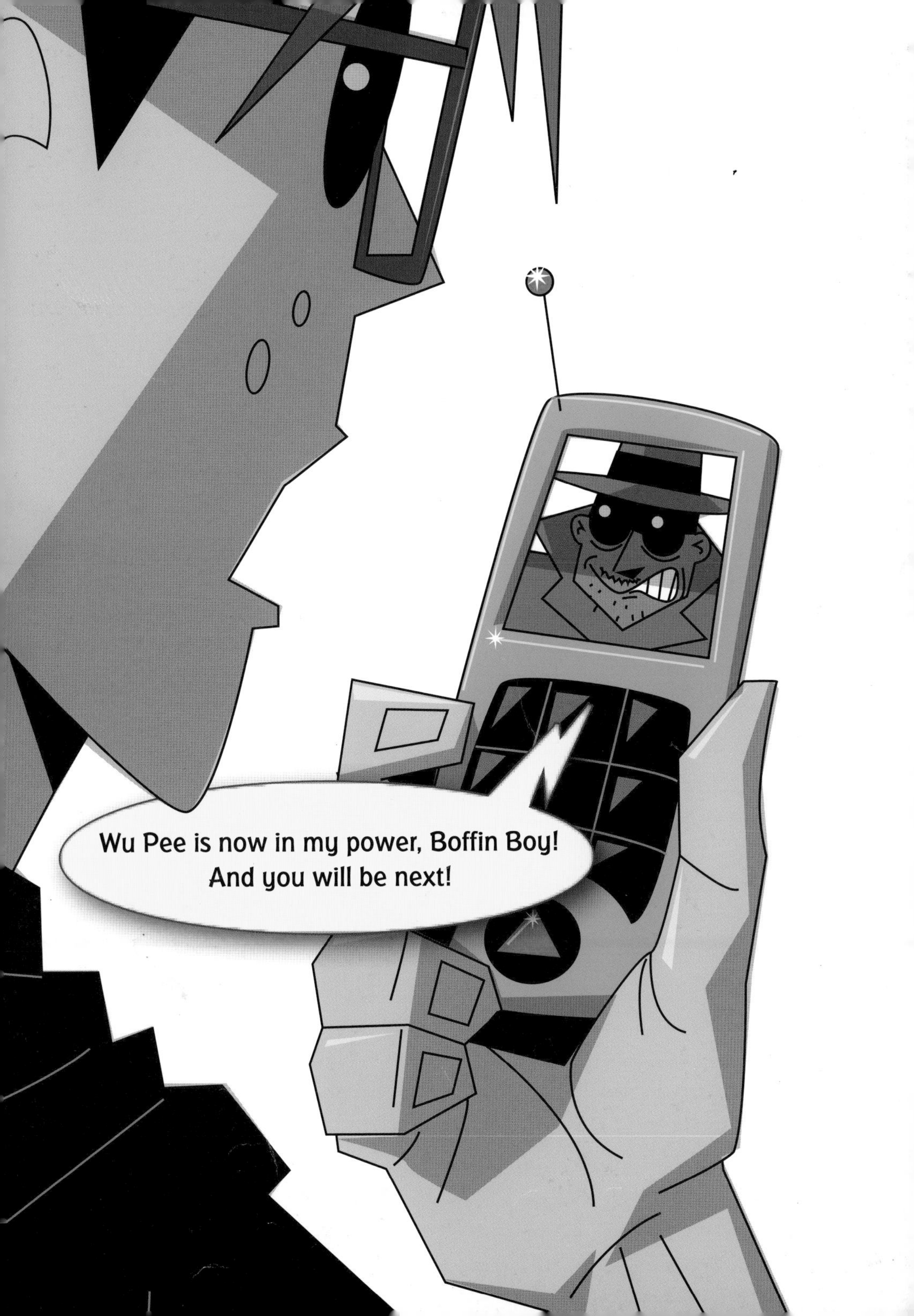
Wu Pee is now in my power, Boffin Boy! And you will be next!

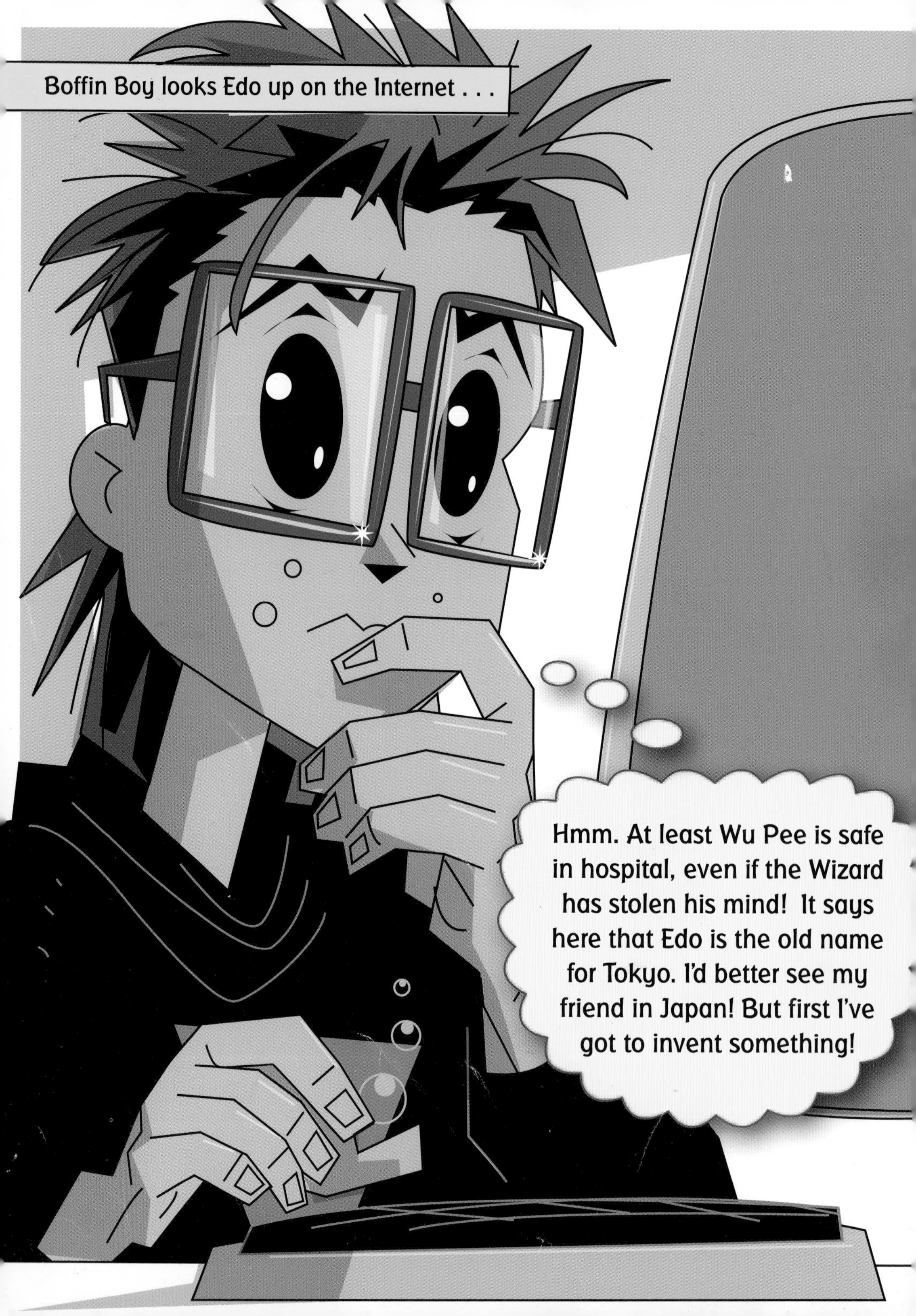
Boffin Boy looks Edo up on the Internet . . .
Hmm. At least Wu Pee is safe in hospital, even if the Wizard has stolen his mind! It says here that Edo is the old name for Tokyo. I'd better see my friend in Japan! But first I've got to invent something!

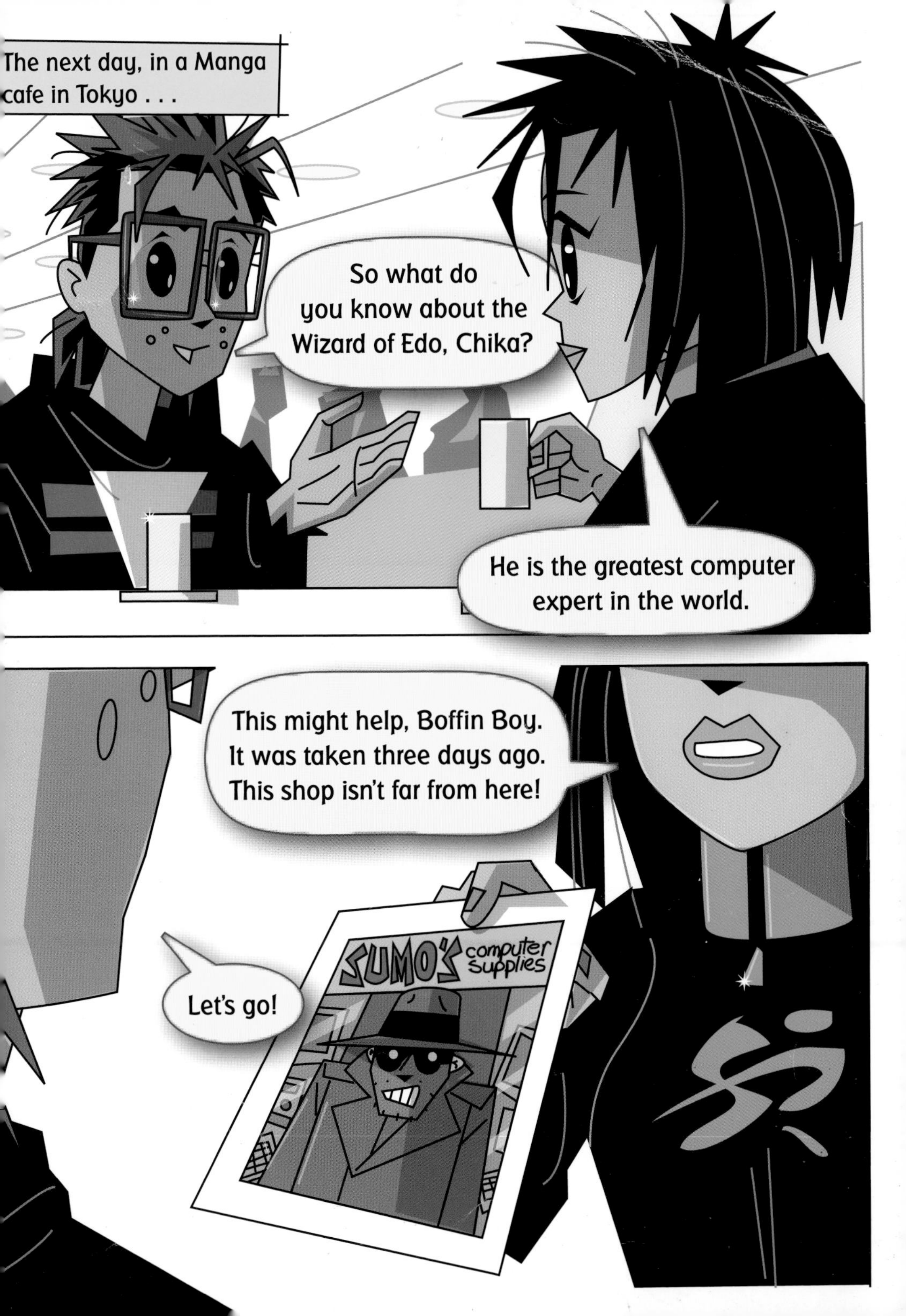
The next day, in a Manga cafe in Tokyo . . .
So what do you know about the Wizard of Edo, Chika?
He is the greatest computer expert in the world.
This might help, Boffin Boy. It was taken three days ago. This shop isn't far from here!
SUMO'S computer supplies
Let's go!

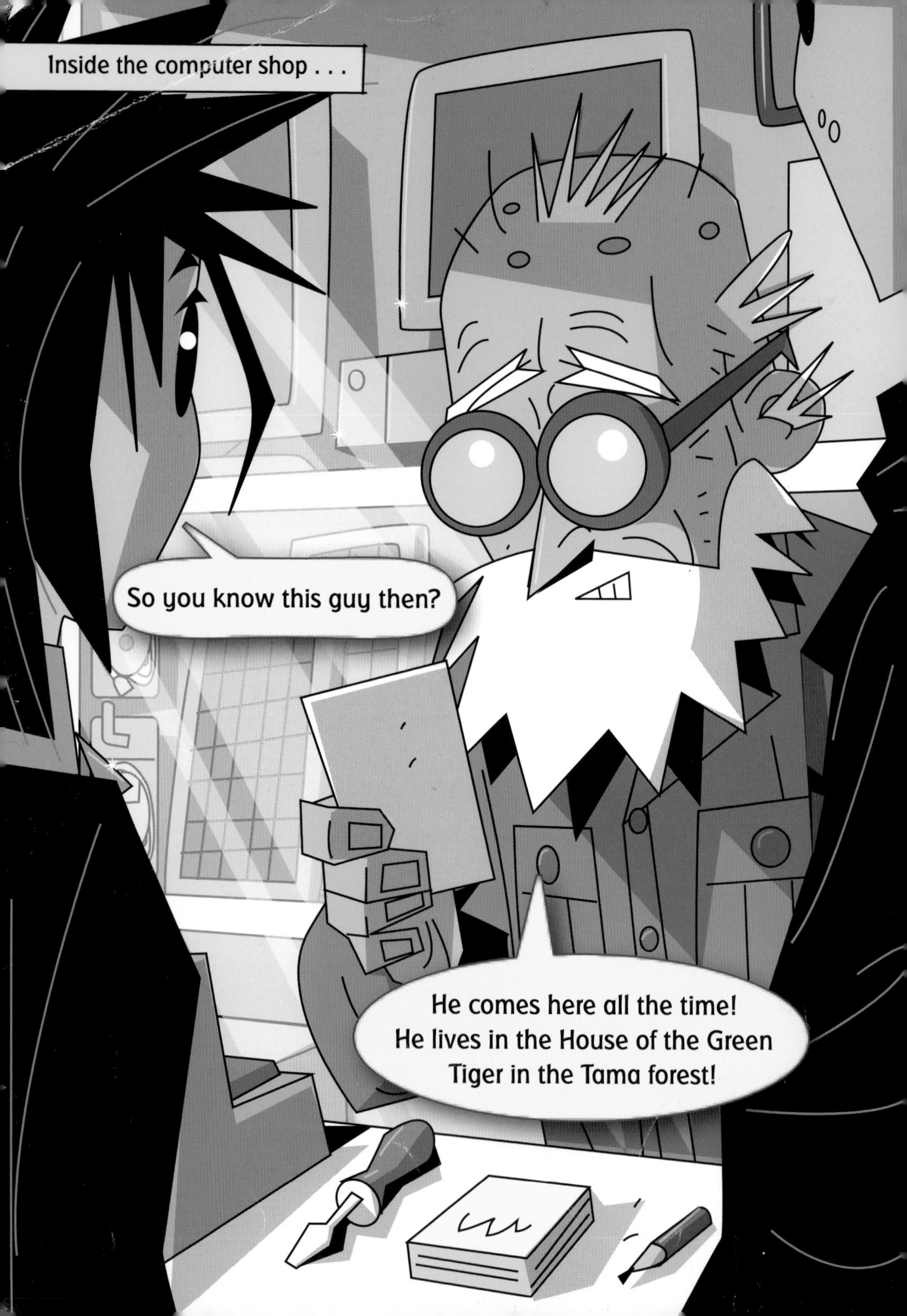
Inside the computer shop . . .
So you know this guy then?
He comes here all the time! He lives in the House of the Green Tiger in the Tama forest!

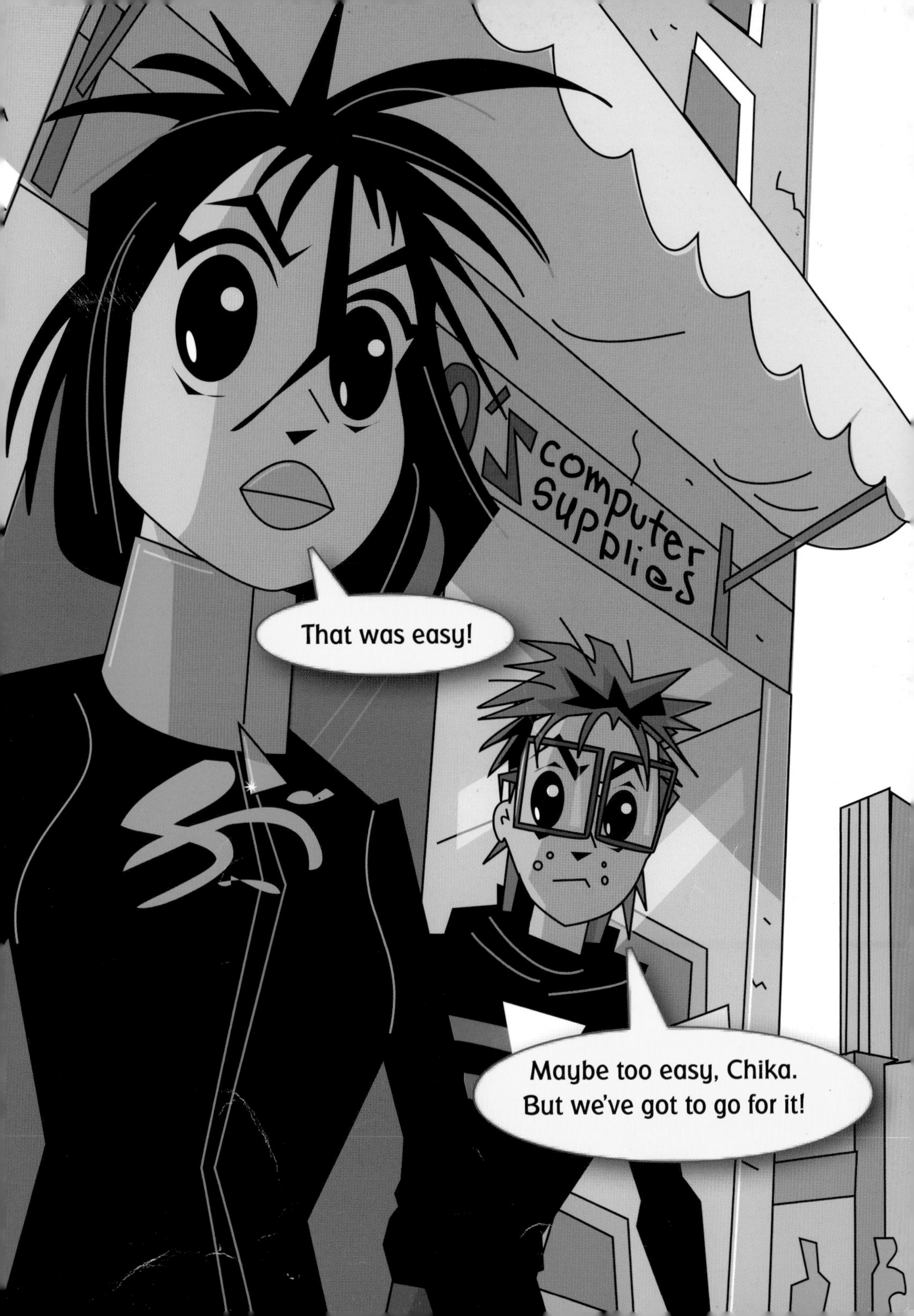
Computer Supplies
That was easy!
Maybe too easy, Chika. But we've got to go for it!

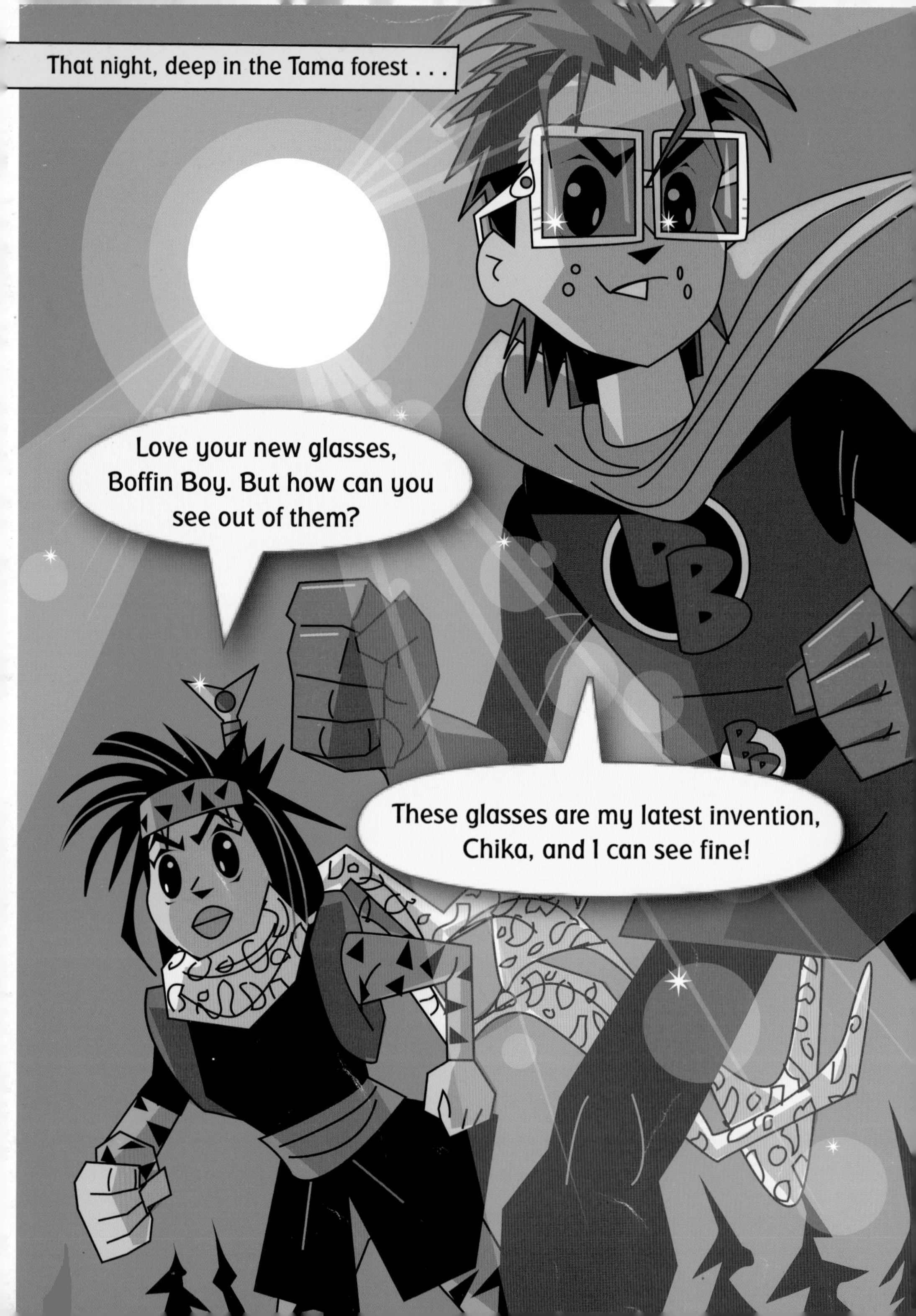
That night, deep in the Tama forest . . .
Love your new glasses, Boffin Boy. But how can you see out of them?
These glasses are my latest invention, Chika, and I can see fine!

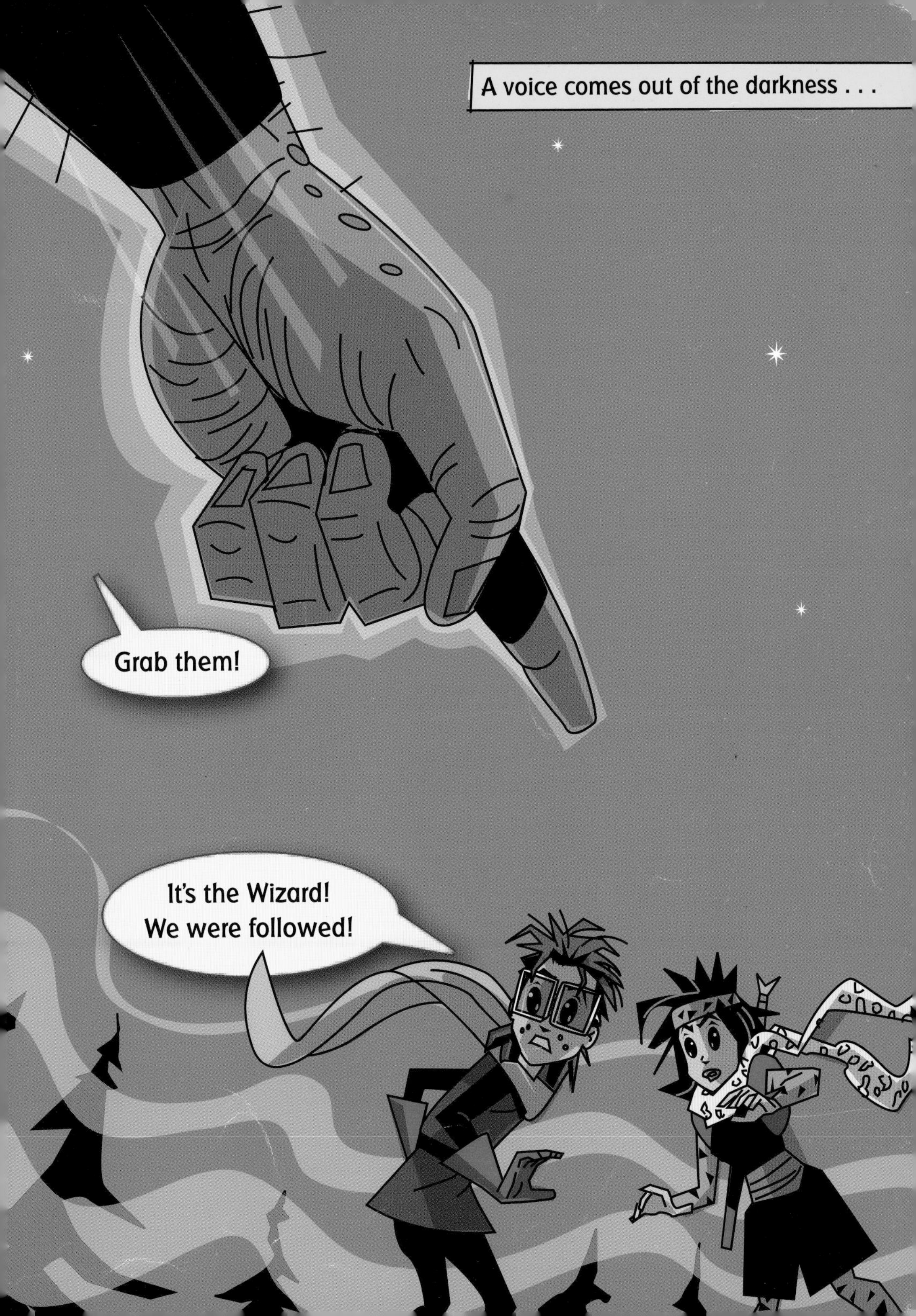
A voice comes out of the darkness . . .
Grab them!
It's the Wizard! We were followed!

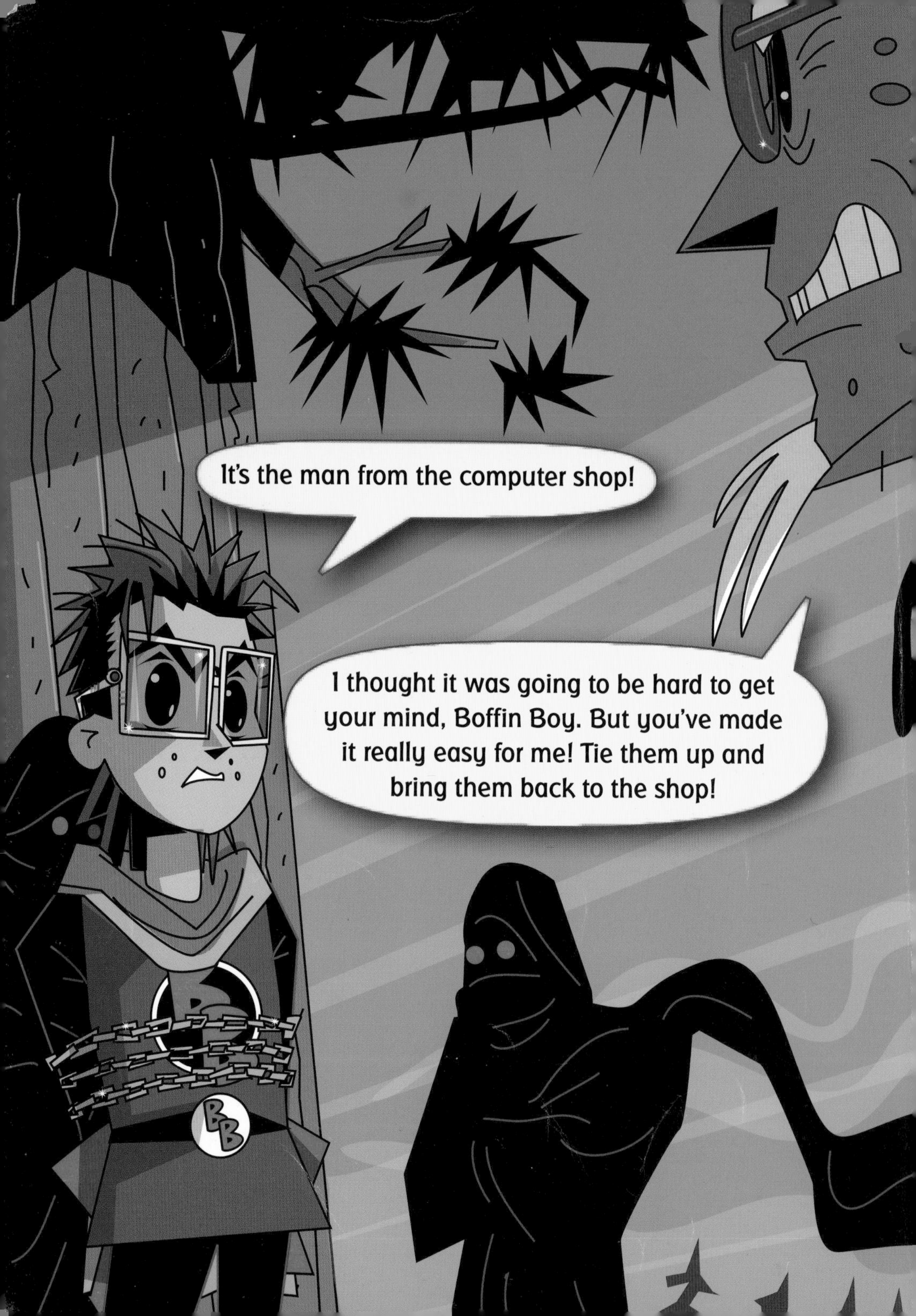
It's the man from the computer shop!
I thought it was going to be hard to get your mind, Boffin Boy. But you've made it really easy for me! Tie them up and bring them back to the shop!

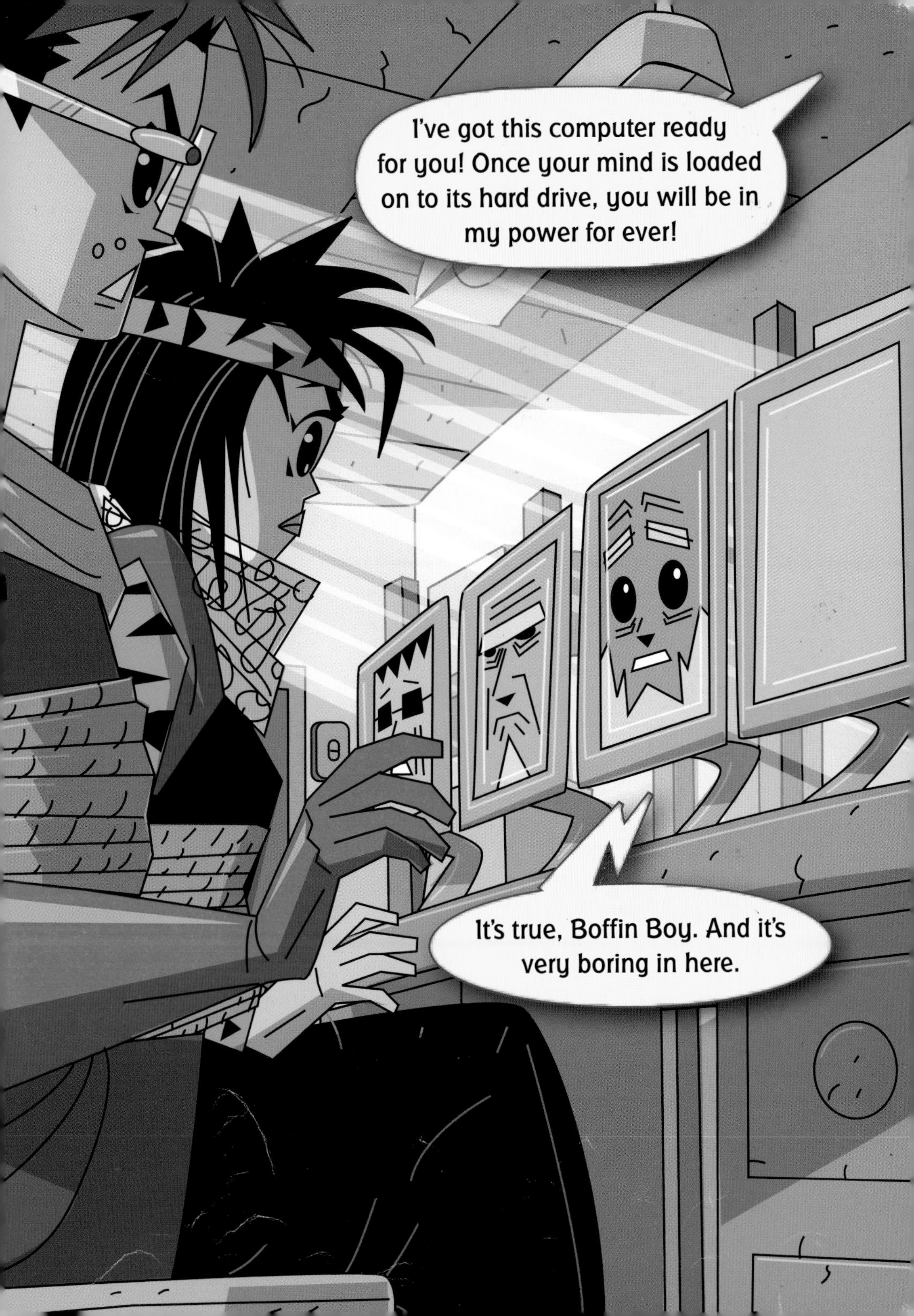
I've got this computer ready for you! Once your mind is loaded on to its hard drive, you will be in my power for ever!
It's true, Boffin Boy. And it's very boring in here.

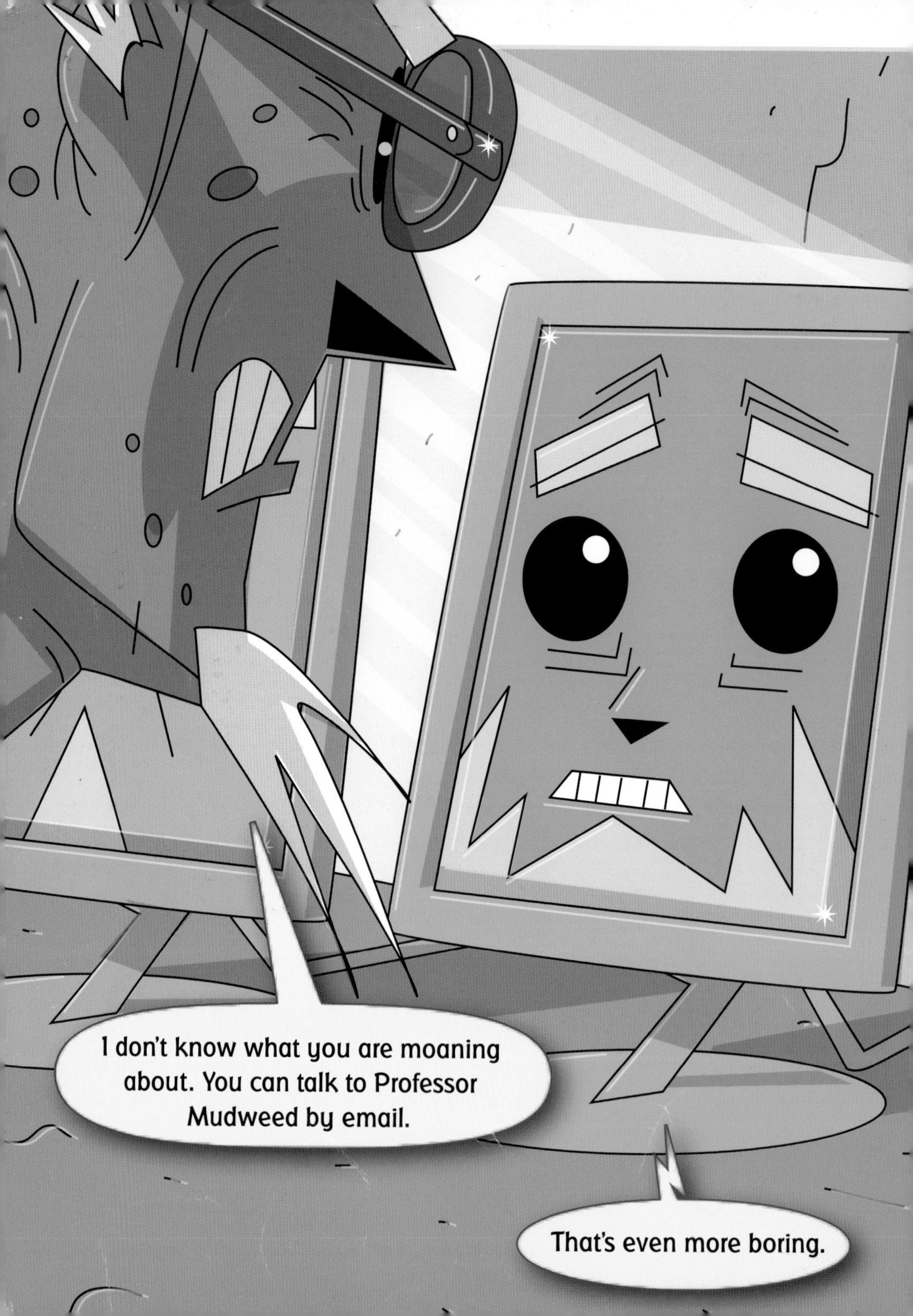
I don't know what you are moaning about. You can talk to Professor Mudweed by email.
That's even more boring.

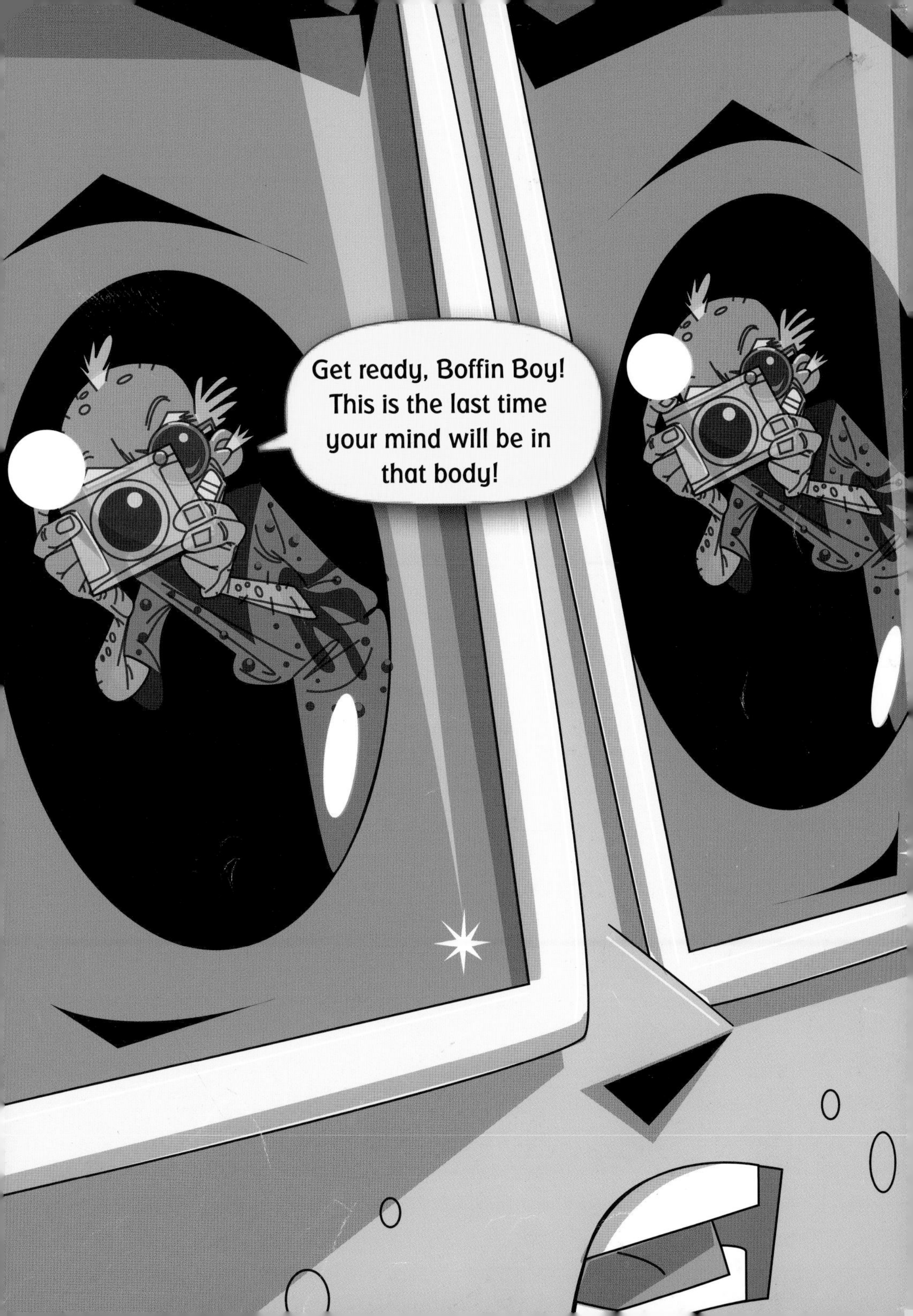
Get ready, Boffin Boy! This is the last time your mind will be in that body!

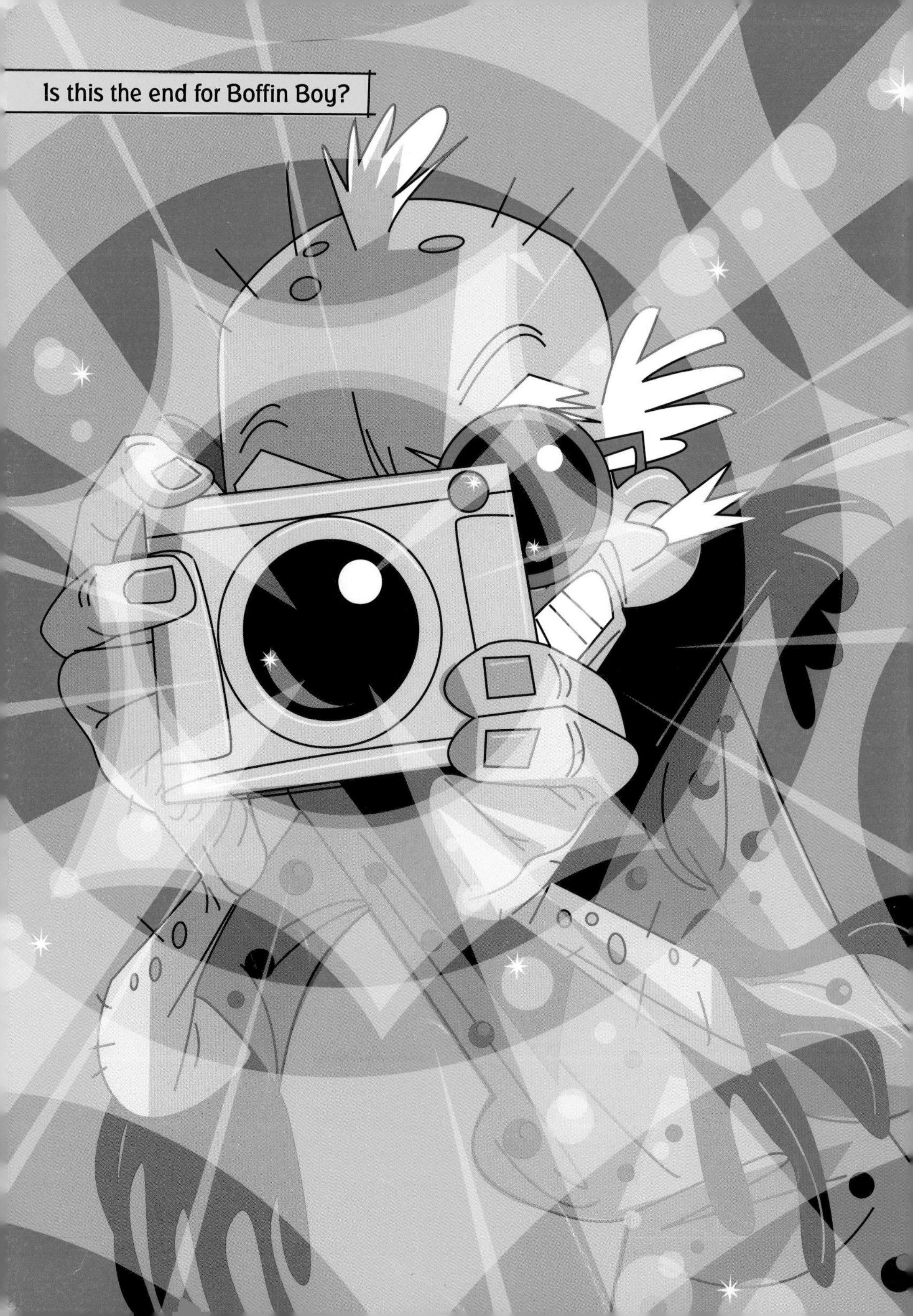
Is this the end for Boffin Boy?

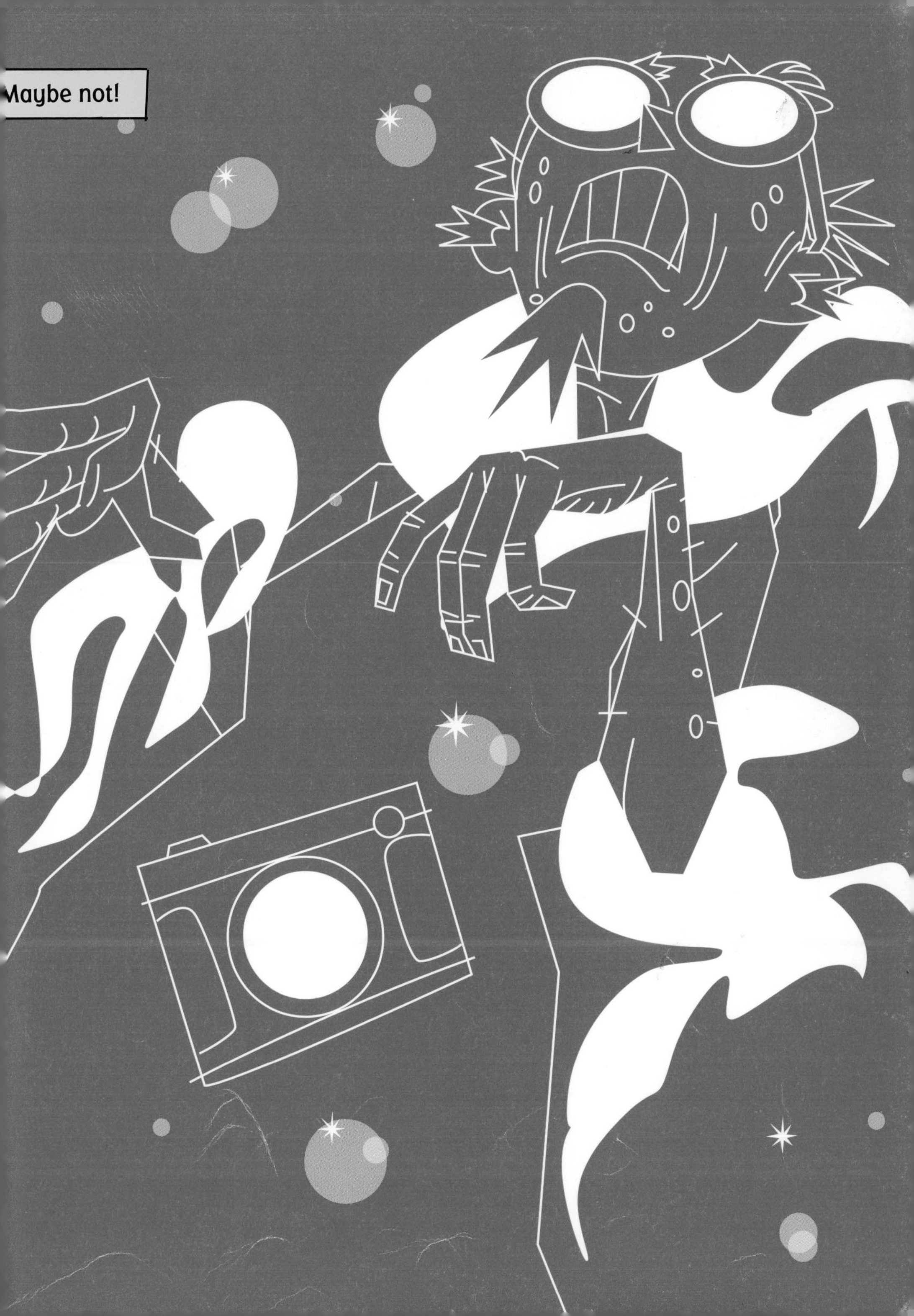
Maybe not!

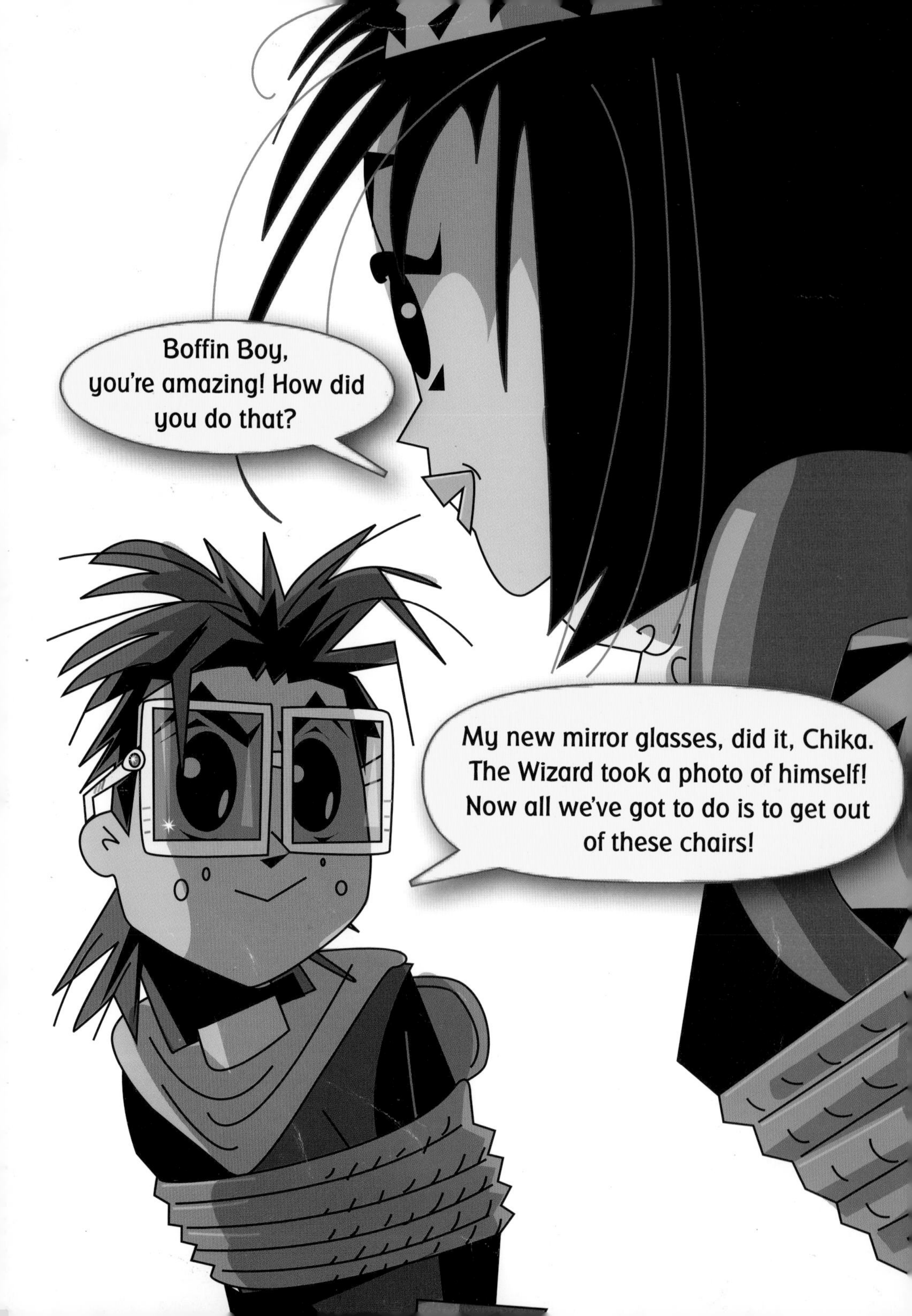
Boffin Boy, you're amazing! How did you do that?
My new mirror glasses, did it, Chika. The Wizard took a photo of himself! Now all we've got to do is to get out of these chairs!

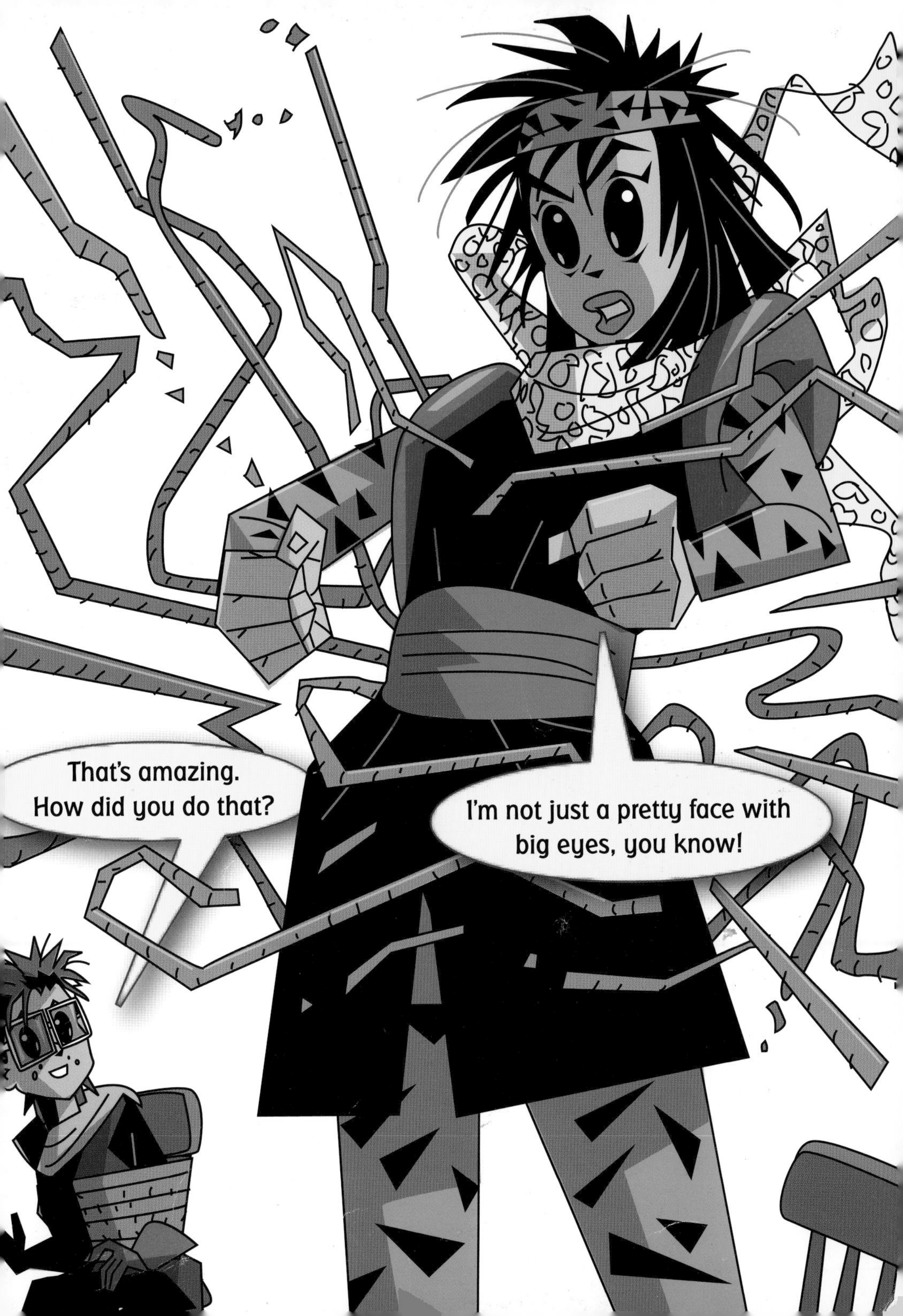
That's amazing. How did you do that?
I'm not just a pretty face with big eyes, you know!

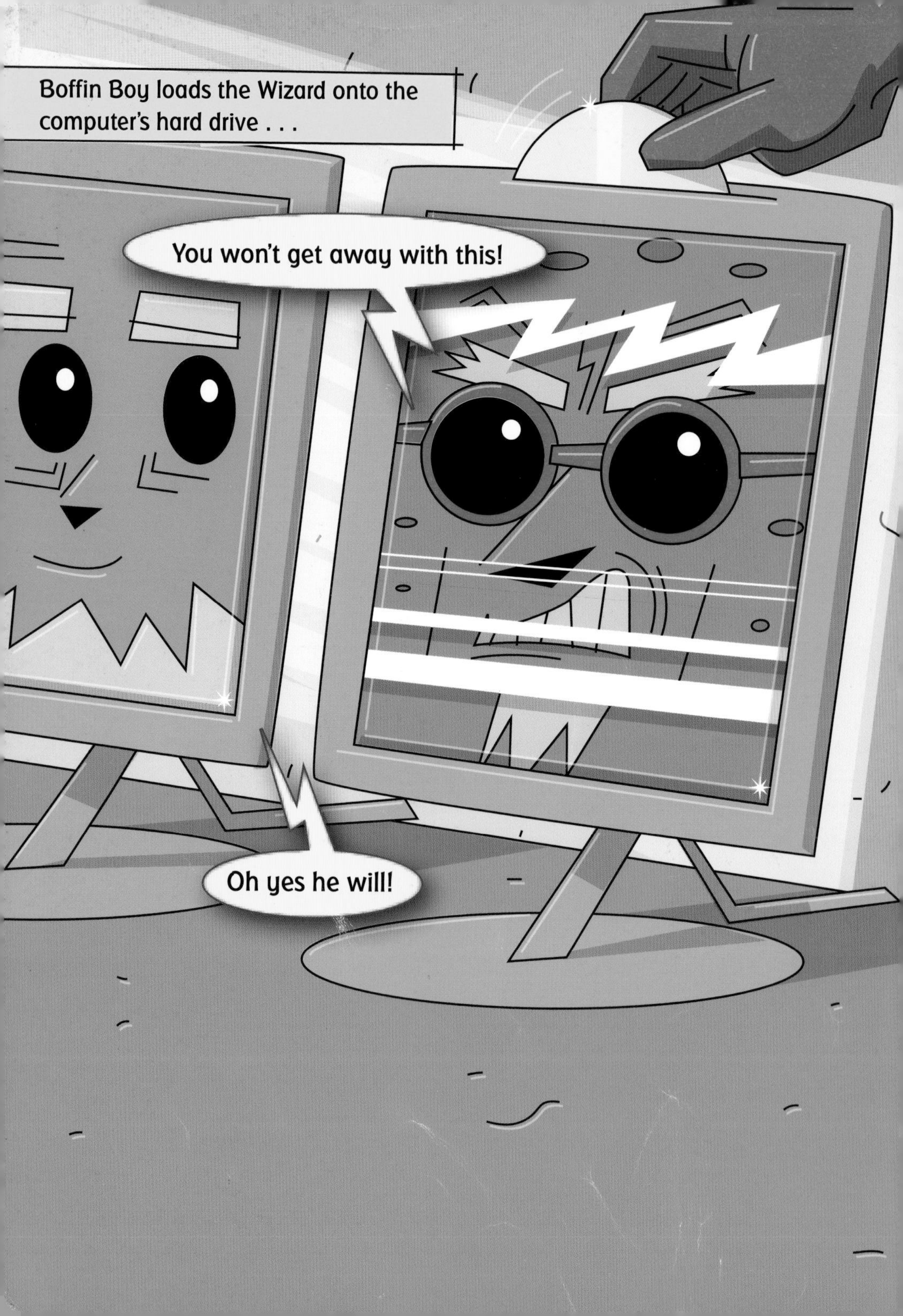
Boffin Boy loads the Wizard onto the computer's hard drive . . .
You won't get away with this!
Oh yes he will!

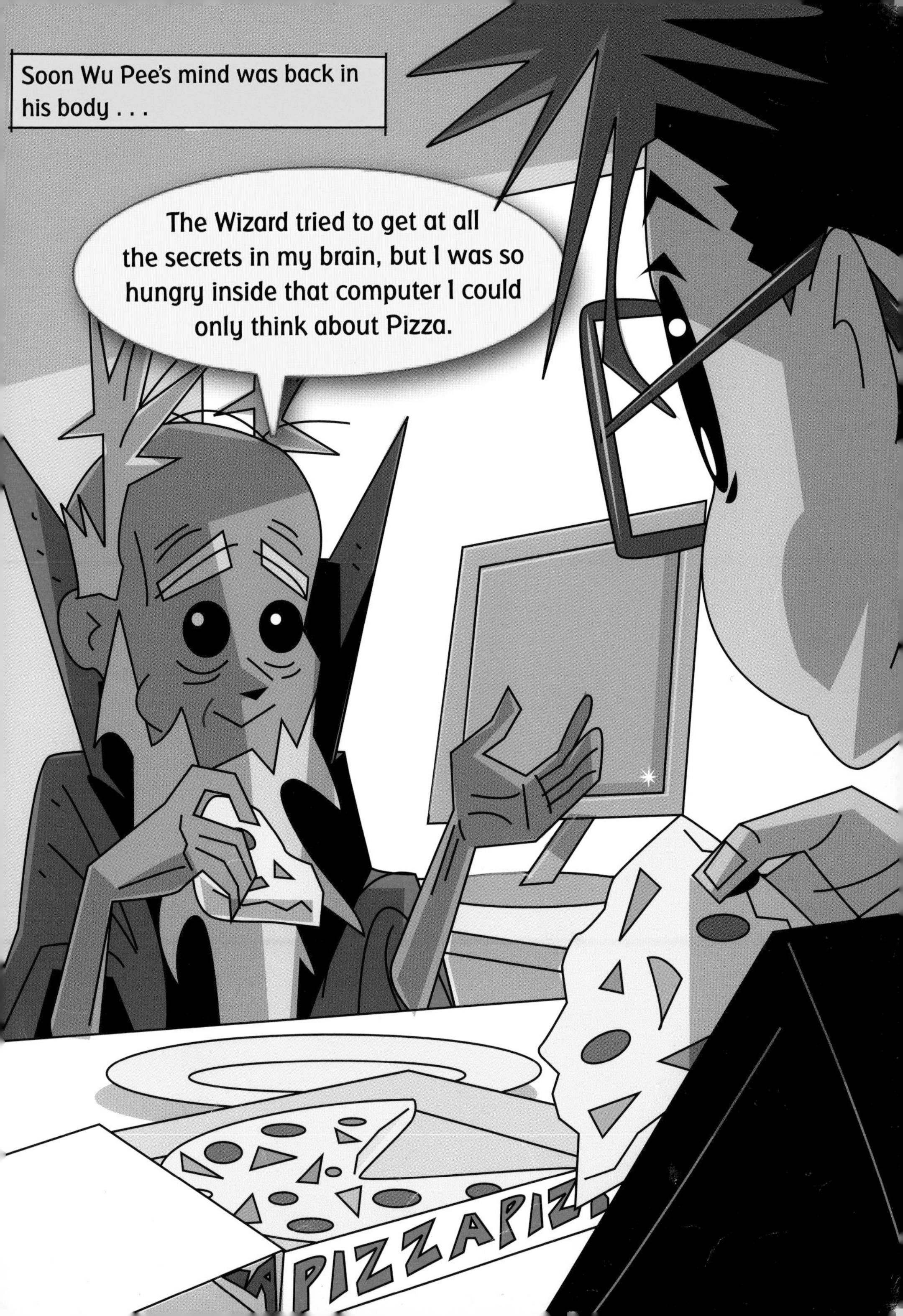
Soon Wu Pee's mind was back in his body . . .
The Wizard tried to get at all the secrets in my brain, but I was so hungry inside that computer I could only think about Pizza.
PIZZAPIZ

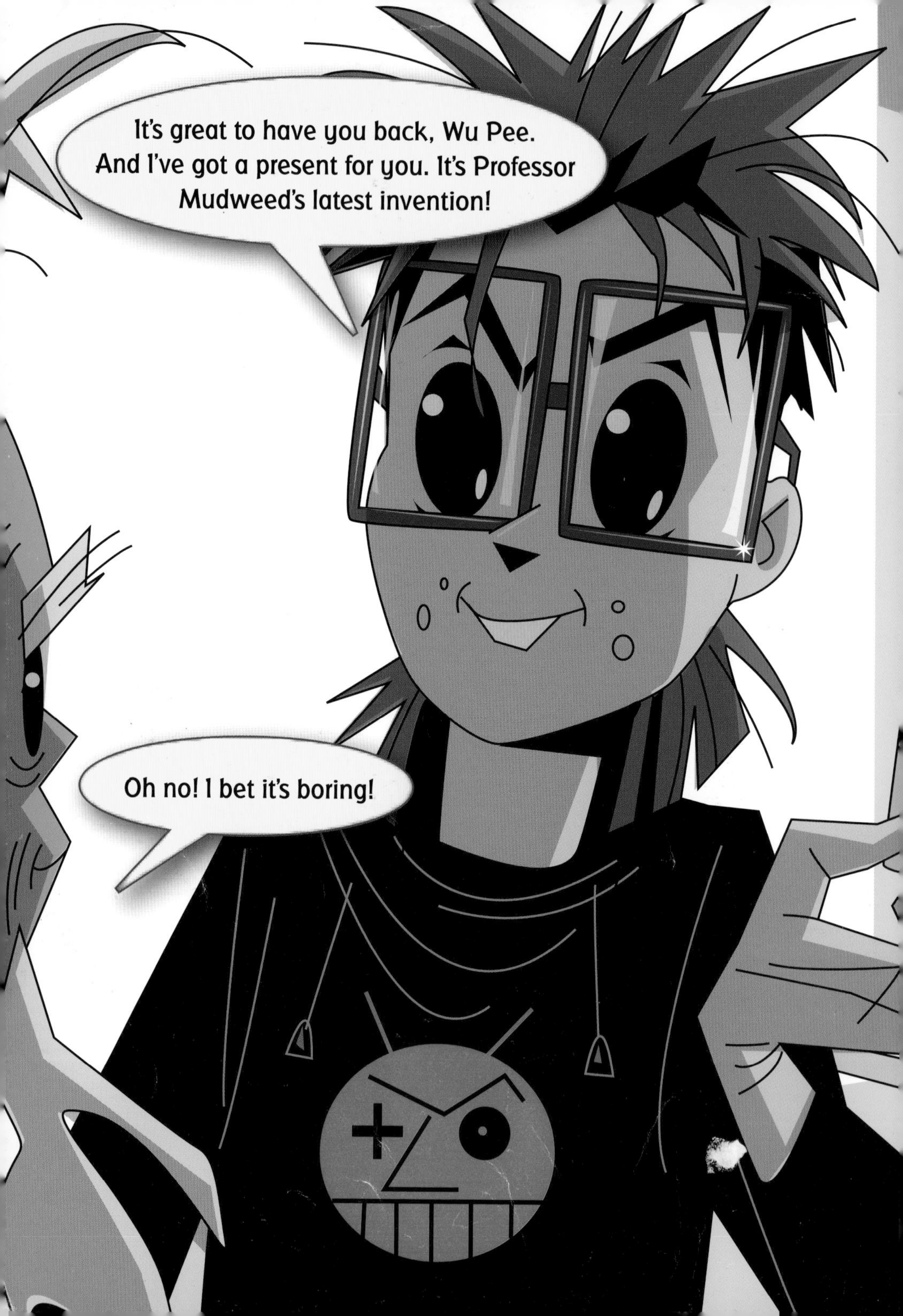
It's great to have you back, Wu Pee. And I've got a present for you. It's Professor Mudweed's latest invention!
Oh no! I bet it's boring!

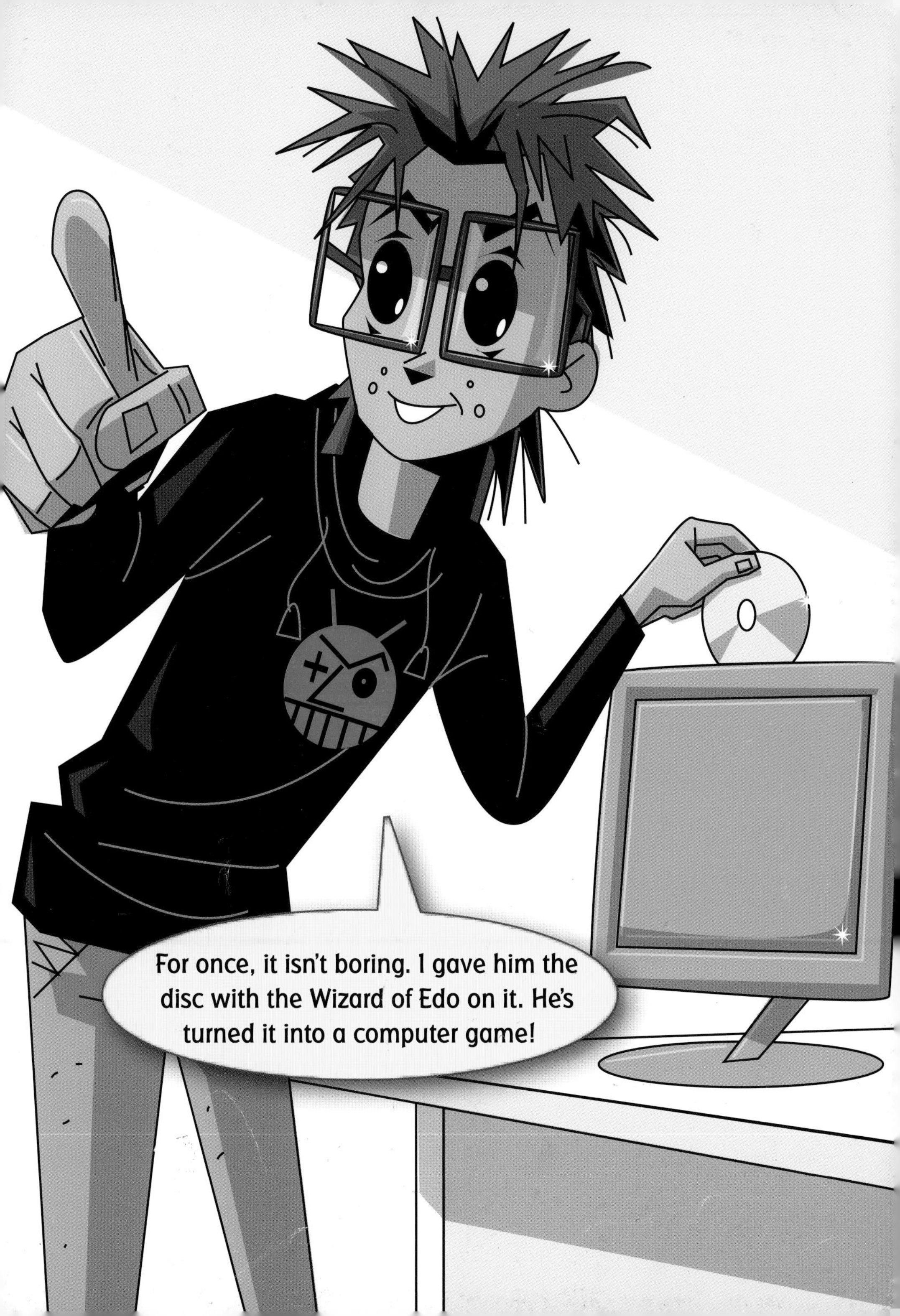
For once, it isn't boring. I gave him the disc with the Wizard of Edo on it. He's turned it into a computer game!

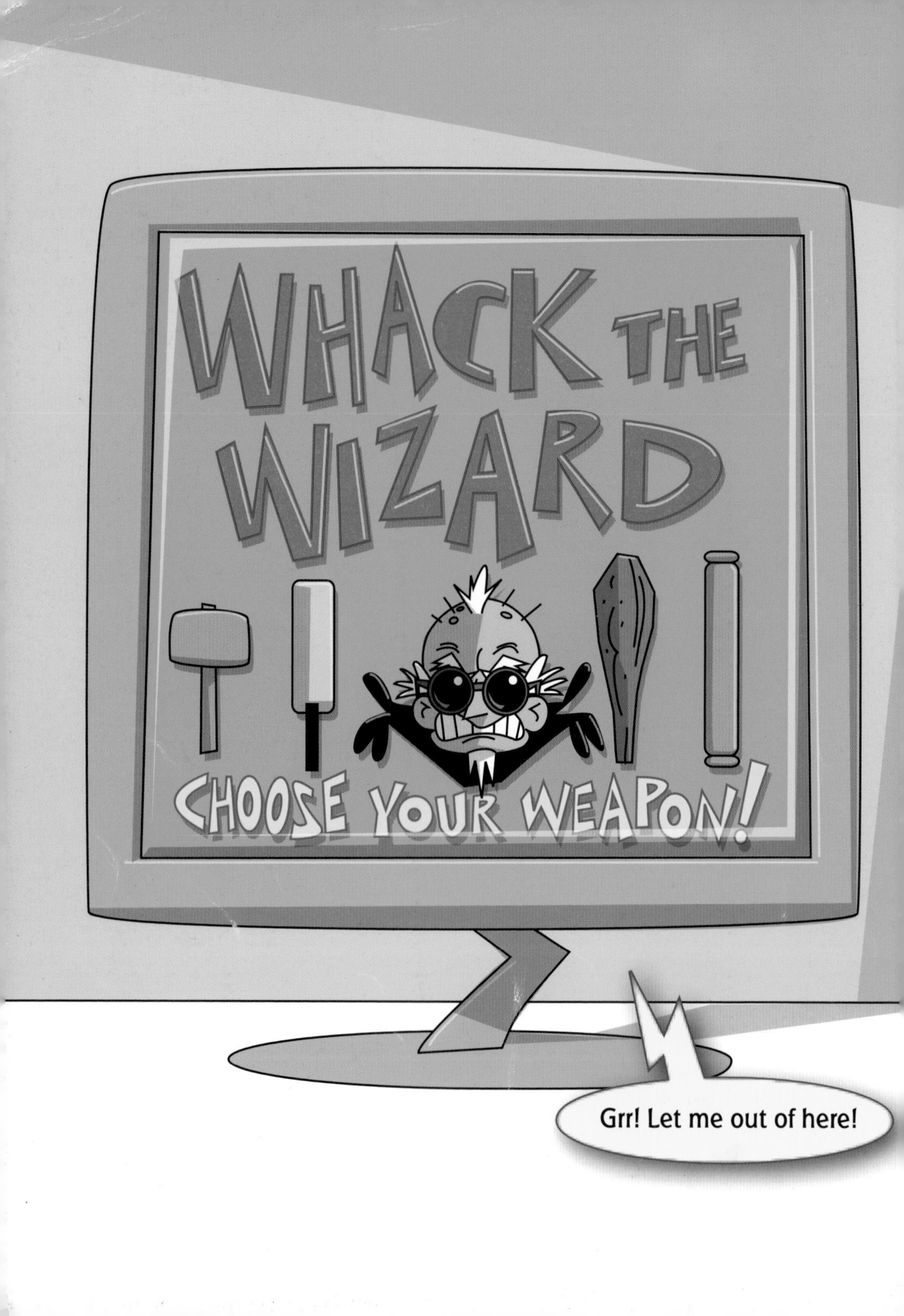
WHACK THE WIZARD
CHOOSE YOUR WEAPON!
Grr! Let me out of here!

ABOUT THE AUTHOR

David Orme has written over 200 books
including poetry collections, fiction and
non-fiction, and school text books. When he
is not writing books he travels around the UK,
giving performances, running writing workshops
and courses.

Find out more at:
www.magic-nation.com.